Praise for Anthony Lamarr's Novels

The Pages We Forget

"Anthony Lamarr's *The Pages We Forget* is certainly not forgettable...The story of innocence lost is an intertwining theme through the lives of three characters. By way of their voices and experiences, along with Lamarr's creative talent, we are invited to feel compassion and joy, anger and hope, and sacrifice and love. Wrapped up in these pages is a celebration of the human spirit." -- *USA Today "Must Read Romance"*

"Lamarr mines his musical background to offer authentic insights into how a song or album transitions from an idea to an actual product. Without giving away spoilers, I will say everyone closely guards secrets in this romantic novel that may require a box of tissues at its conclusion." -- *Library Journal*

"Touching, suspenseful love story...Likely to appeal to those who enjoy the novels of Nicholas Sparks...I choked up with tears as the novel progressed toward its inevitable climax." -- *Tallahassee Democrat*

Our First Love

"Romantic love and family devotion dominate the heart of Lamarr's literary novels...Remarkable for its careful rendering of an intense first love and for the deep bonds of brotherly love unique to this novel...*Our First Love* stayed with me long after the final pages." -- *Southern Literary Review*

"5 Stars...Fantastic...An amazing read." -- *Book Referees*

"There's such richness in the narrative layers...Pick this up if you enjoy books that stick with you for days after you've finished reading them." -- *To Each Their Own Book Reviews*

ALSO BY ANTHONY LAMARR

Novels
Our First Love
The Pages We Forget

Plays
Calming the Man
The Long Goodbye

EVERY YEAR, EVERY

Christmas

A Novel

ANTHONY LAMARR

Antmar Books
USA

For
My Mother
Delores "Lois" White

"I will wait for you today,
tomorrow, and always."

Anthony Lamarr

EVERY YEAR, EVERY
Christmas

Christmas

Chapter 1

Snow was in the forecast.

The previous winter's dusting of snow and ice brought the city to a standstill. Black ice on the unsalted highways caused vehicles to slip, slide, and spin out of control. The collisions led to pileups that eventually brought traffic to a halt across the city. Lanes of stalled vehicles stretched for miles, forcing most of the drivers and occupants to spend the day and night inside their vehicles. A few abandoned their vehicles and chanced making it on foot through the two inches of snow.

Bryant Fuller took a chance that day. After leaving work and getting as close as a mile and a half from his apartment, he found himself in a traffic jam that stretched nearly two miles in front of him and was rapidly extending behind him. Radio hosts on every local station warned drivers of the hazardous conditions and advised them to take their time and be careful on the icy roads. Their advice to drivers who were already stranded was to stay warm and safe. Upon hearing this, Bryant pressed the ignition button to turn off the car. He laughed to himself and then out loud. A native of Chicago, it was his first winter in Atlanta, and he was stuck on the highway gazing out the window and wondering how such a small amount of snow could create so much havoc.

He was working as a reporter for a weekly newspaper in Chicago when he responded to a job announcement for the *Marietta Daily Journal*. The Metro Atlanta newspaper was looking for an experienced news and features writer. Bryant had considered moving to Atlanta, a hotspot for young, black professionals, when he graduated from college, but he decided to stay close to home so he could help his mother with his twin brother and sister, Taylor and Talia, who were still in high school. After Taylor and Talia finished their freshman year of college, Bryant felt it was time for him to make a move. He submitted his resume and portfolio on a Monday. The next day, Otis Murphy, the newspaper's managing editor, called to conduct a phone interview. Bryant was anticipating Otis' first question: Why do you want to relocate to Atlanta?

"Atlanta is growing, and I want to be part of that growth," he responded. "Professionally and personally."

Otis asked about his education and work experience.

"I graduated from Illinois State with a bachelor's degree in journalism five years ago," he answered. "I landed a job as a crime beat reporter for the Defender three weeks later. A year later, I moved to features, which is where I am now."

They discussed some of the articles in Bryant's portfolio.

An in-depth series on the city's opioid epidemic. A feature about a seventy-five-year love affair between an elderly couple who started dating in high school. A personality profile of the city's new mayor. And a series on the lack of access to quality healthcare and medical services for some Chicago inner-city communities.

Then Otis asked when he could start.

"In three weeks," he said. "I need to give my editor a two-week notice, and I need a week to relocate."

Two days later, during Sunday dinner at his mother's house, Bryant told his family – his mother, Felicia, his older sister Samantha and her husband Kyle, and Taylor and Talia. "I accepted a position at a daily in Atlanta Friday, so I'll be moving at the end of the month," he announced.

"I didn't know you were looking for a job in Atlanta," Taylor said.

"Neither did I," his mother followed.

"Isn't that something," Talia snapped. "You talked me out of applying to Spelman, and now you're taking off to Atlanta."

"That's because you're nineteen, and you need to be close enough for Mom to reach out and touch you when she needs to," he shot back.

"Your brother's right," Felicia backed Bryant. "When you graduate from college, and I see that you can handle being on your own…"

Talia cut her off. "I already live on my own."

"You don't live on your own," Samantha chimed in. "You stay in a college dorm ten minutes from here."

"Slow down. You're speeding," Talia quipped. "It's twenty-two minutes if you drive the speed limit."

"I told you I was the smart twin," Taylor interjected. "And if you ask me, I don't think she'll ever be ready to live on her own."

"I know the boy who still lives at home with his mother isn't talking," Talia shot back.

"The reason I can talk is because I'm not trying to go anywhere," Taylor revealed what everyone already knew. "I'm staying right here with my favorite girl. And, when the urge hits me to get away for a bit, I'll visit my big brother in Atlanta."

"I'm going to hold you to that," Bryant said.

Two months after Bryant moved, Taylor made good on his promise and flew down to Atlanta during his college's spring break. Taylor planned to visit again last Christmas too, but Bryant wasn't ready to spend his first Christmas away from home. So, he told Taylor he was coming home for Christmas.

Bryant was scheduled to work this Christmas, so he had not made plans to go home. That was until the week before Thanksgiving when his co-worker John asked if they could switch schedules. Bryant was scheduled to be off Thanksgiving. John was scheduled to be off Christmas, but he wanted to switch so he could be home with his pregnant wife, Lacey, whose due date was the Wednesday before Thanksgiving. Bryant agreed. The next day he booked a Christmas Eve flight from Atlanta to Chicago.

Four days before Christmas, his plans changed again.

The newsroom staff was taking a two-hour afternoon break for its office Christmas party and to exchange gifts. Bryant had drawn Katie's name and gotten her a Walmart gift card. Bryant, John, and sports reporter Cal Reaves were sitting at a table in the breakroom when Otis and Susan, the newspaper's editorial writer, handed them their gifts. Susan had pulled Bryant's name and gotten him a scarf, gloves, and earmuffs.

"I figured you'll need those when you get to Chicago," Susan said to Bryant as she walked away from the table.

"You're going to wish you had kept them for yourself," Otis said. "I just heard the weather forecast. It's supposed to snow Christmas Eve."

"It can't snow," Bryant blurted. "I'm flying to Chicago Christmas Eve."

"If I were you, I'd try to get an earlier flight," John said. "You remember what happened the last time it snowed here."

Later that afternoon, as Bryant sat at his desk waiting for the airline's customer service representative to return to the phone, he remembered the last time the forecast was for snow in Atlanta. Less than three inches of snow paralyzed the city and stranded him and hundreds of other motorists on the city's streets and highways. Bryant recalled his decision to pull his car out of the traffic lane to the side of the highway, lock the doors, then walk the mile and a half to his apartment. It wasn't a Chicago snowstorm, but it started to feel like it. The light jacket he wore could not keep the snow and frigid winds at bay. By the time he arrived at his apartment – nearly an hour later, he could barely walk. His frozen feet had to be pried out his shoes.

Several minutes passed before the customer service representative returned to the phone and told Bryant the only available flight was the next day – the day before Christmas Eve. Bryant rescheduled his flight. Leaving a day earlier than expected meant he had to rush to finish packing, but he didn't mind. He just wanted to get out of Atlanta before the snow fell and shut the city down again.

Chapter 2

It was supposed to be Bryant's first Christmas away from home.

As he stared out the airplane window at the clouds below, he thought about what his Christmas would have been like if he and John had not switched schedules. Instead of flying to Chicago to spend the holiday with his family, he would be preparing to spend Christmas Eve alone in the newsroom since he would've been the only reporter working and the copy editors didn't come in until two. If snow had not shut down the city by the time he clocked out, he would've met Cal at Caesar's Sports Bar to play pool and have a few too many drinks. After waking from a drunken sleep, he would've spent Christmas morning staring out the window at the tidbits of snow left on the ground and wondering if a pair of jeans and a sweater were too casual for dinner at John's house. The rest of the day would be spent wishing he were home.

He had not been home since last Christmas, so he was ready to spend time catching up with his family. He was ready to meet his seven-month old nephew, Kyle Jr., Samantha and Kyle's son. His mom, Felicia, had retired in June after teaching high school English for thirty-five years, and he was ready to see if she was as happy about retirement as she sounded on the phone. She had retired in June after teaching high school English for thirty-five years. He was ready to check out the apartment Talia moved into during the summer, and he was ready to hang out with Taylor for a night or two of bar hopping and cutting the fool with some of his friends.

Bryant managed to get out of Atlanta before the forecasted two-to-three inches of snow crippled the city, but snow was in the forecast for Chicago, too. The city was still digging its way out the three feet of snow dumped by a blizzard the previous week. Another foot of snow was expected to fall between Christmas Eve and Christmas Day.

Taylor was waiting in his black Mustang at the curb when Bryant walked out of O'Hare International Airport carrying his luggage. Taylor blew the horn to get Bryant's attention. If not for the six years separating them, Bryant and Taylor could have been twins. So, Bryant was a bit surprised when he turned and saw Taylor, who was sporting a neatly trimmed goatee, which made the two of them look even more alike.

"Do you know who you look like now that you've sprouted some facial hair?" Bryant asked as he walked up to the car.

"As long as I don't look like you, I'm okay," Taylor responded. "What you got me for Christmas?" Taylor pressed the button to open the trunk.

"The usual," Bryant answered as he put his luggage in the trunk.

"What do you mean, the usual?"

"The usual." Bryant got in the car, closed the door, then put on his seatbelt.

"Man, I hope you didn't buy everybody gift cards this year."

"What's wrong with gift cards?" Bryant asked.

"There's nothing wrong with gift cards," Taylor responded. "Just don't give me one on Christmas. I'll take them on my birthday or any other day, but on Christmas, I want presents. Everybody does."

Taylor steered the car into the traffic lane.

"Mom smiled and thanked you for her gift card last Christmas, but she wasn't too happy about it."

"Did she tell you that?"

"She didn't have to," Taylor replied. "I know her."

Bryant knew Taylor was telling the truth, which meant he needed to get up early the next morning and use the gift cards to buy actual gifts for everyone.

"So, what do you think about the new ride?" Taylor asked.

"I love it," Bryant answered. "But now I'm wondering how much you make working part-time."

"About fifty grand," he disclosed. "And guess what? They've already offered me a full-time computer engineering position after graduation."

Felicia was waiting for them at the house. When she saw Taylor pull in the driveway, she opened the front door and hurried outside. As soon as Taylor put the car in park, Bryant jumped out and raced over to her.

"My baby's home," she cried and threw her arms around him.

Taylor got out the car correcting her, "Mom, he's your boy. I'm your baby."

"You're right," she responded. "My big boy's home." She opened the front door. "Let's go inside and get out this cold."

"Bryant!" Taylor called. "Don't you wanna get your luggage first?"

"You can bring it in for him," she said and guided Bryant inside in front of her.

"Man, come get your luggage!" Taylor yelled as the front door closed behind them.

The house was filled with familiar holiday scents. Fresh pine in the living room. In the kitchen – the sweet smell of apples, cinnamon, and cookies baking in the oven. The aromatic fragrance of sweet holiday candles wafted throughout the upstairs hallway, bedrooms, and bathrooms.

Bryant inhaled deeply then exhaled. "It feels and smells good to be home," he said.

Family and friends regarded Bryant as the mature, serious brother and Taylor as the cool, fun brother. This didn't bother Bryant at first. He was expected to be more mature and serious. He was several years older than Taylor, and he became the man of the house when their father died nine years ago. However, after Taylor graduated from high school and began doing grown-up things, like going out, dating, and cutting the fool, Bryant secretly wished he could be more outgoing like his little brother. Bryant got his wish one evening when he stopped by his mother's house and Taylor was getting ready to go to a friend's house party. Bryant was surprised when Taylor asked if he wanted to come, but he wasn't surprised by his response, "Let's go." Bryant turned and followed Taylor out the door without letting his mother know he had been there. That night was the first time Taylor had seen Bryant get drunk, get loose, and cut the fool. Bryant wasn't pleased with his behavior, so a week later, he began growing a goatee, hoping it would make him look and act older.

Taylor had already made plans for him and Bryant to meet a few friends at Champs, a neighborhood bar and lounge near their mother's house. Talia, had to work late, but was going to meet them at the bar. Taylor was dressed and downstairs waiting for Bryant, who was getting dressed in Talia's old bedroom.

Before moving to Atlanta, Bryant packed some of his winterwear in the closet, which was crammed with clothes Talia didn't take with her when she moved in the dorm. Bryant pulled a black leather jacket off a hanger in the back of the closet. He bought the Tom Ford leather jacket from Bloomingdales the winter before he moved to Atlanta. It fit like it was custom made for him. He thought about taking the jacket to Atlanta, but he felt it would hardly ever be cold enough in Atlanta to wear it. So, he packed the jacket, a heavy hooded coat, and a few pair of snow boots in the closet. He was coming down the stairs when Taylor turned and saw him.

"Where did you hide it?" Taylor asked.

"Hide what?"

"That jacket," Taylor answered. "I've been looking for it since you left last Christmas."

"It was behind a bunch of Talia's things," Bryant said. "Are you ready?"

"I was ready twenty minutes ago," Taylor replied and started toward the door. "Mom! Don't wait up for your baby," he yelled.

"I'm not." She walked to the top of the stairway and smiled at her sons. "You just make sure you get my boy back here safe and sound."

"Don't worry," Taylor assured her. "I got my big brother."

"I love you, Mom," Bryant yelled back to her as he closed the door behind him and Taylor.

An hour later, Bryant was sitting at a table in Champs with Taylor and his friends Richard, Darryl, and Koran playing a holiday drinking game, "Here We Come Drinking and Caroling." They were singing "Rudolph the Red Nose Reindeer." Richard started by singing the first phrase. Darryl, beside Richard, sang the next phrase. It went on this way until it was Bryant's turn. Bryant was downing his third shot of tequila after losing three straights rounds. He knew the lyrics to "Rudolph the Red Nose Reindeer," and he was sure he had not messed up, at least not three straight times. But Taylor and the other guys said he did. After losing a fourth time, Bryant called it quits.

Bryant had just about reached his level when Talia showed up with Jennifer, her new roommate. Talia and Jennifer met a year earlier when they took the same accounting course and were assigned to the same study group. They were both living in a dorm at the time. During the summer, they decided to become roommates and rented an apartment together. Taylor met Jennifer one Sunday when she came to the house with Talia. He didn't pay her too much attention that day, but something happened the next time he saw her. He was helping Talia move into the apartment when Jennifer drove up. She got out the car, shot him a come-hither look as she walked past him, then whispered hello. He wasn't imagining she was flirting with him. Talia saw it too. So, he flirted back. Bryant was still sober enough to see there was something between Taylor and Jennifer. His suspicions were confirmed when Taylor introduced Jennifer to him before Talia could.

It felt good to be home, especially when it was supposed to be his first Christmas away from home. To celebrate, Bryant drank two more Bud Lights and downed another shot of tequila. That ended his night. At least that was the last thing he remembered the next morning.

Chapter 3

Bryant forgot to set the alarm on his cell phone. He wasn't surprised though. He didn't remember coming home, climbing the stairs to the bedroom, or falling to sleep with his pants, shirt, and socks on. When he woke up, it took a few seconds for him to realize where he was – at his mom's house, in his sister's old bedroom. He looked around the room. The black leather jacket he wore was hanging in the closet. His shoes were in the closet too. That meant Taylor had tucked him in last night.

Bryant's plan was to wake up early so he could go exchange the gift cards he had gotten everyone for Christmas and buy real presents. It was Christmas Eve, which meant the stores would be closing early. He looked at the clock beside the bed. 10:18.

The bedroom door was cracked open. It was the smell of bacon and waffles that woke him up. And it made him hungry. He could hear Taylor and his mom talking downstairs. He couldn't discern what they were saying, but he was sure his mom was scolding Taylor for letting his big brother get so drunk that he had to be helped inside and to bed.

Bryant pulled himself up on the edge of the bed, then he sat there for a few minutes waiting for the room to stop spinning. When he was able to stand, he walked, dragging his feet, over to the window.

Snow was falling as forecasted.

As he gazed out the window, he wished he could exchange the thunderous pounding inside his head and Taylor yelling to tell him breakfast was ready for the quietude outside his window. Bryant used his cell phone to text Taylor and let him know he would be down after he took a shower. He walked in the bathroom, turned on the shower, took two Tylenols from a bottle in the medicine cabinet, then undressed and stepped in the stream of rejuvenating water.

Taylor and his mom were sitting at the table when Bryant entered the dining room already dressed to go shopping. Taylor looked at Bryant and said, "I forgot to tell you."

"Tell me what?"

"That we don't dress up for breakfast anymore," Taylor joked.

Bryant walked over to his mom, who had finished eating breakfast but was still sitting at the head of the table. He kissed her on the jaw and said, "Good morning."

"Good morning," she replied. "I put your breakfast in the oven to stay warm." She walked out the dining room to the kitchen.

"Where are you about to go?" Taylor asked.

"I need to pick up a few things before the stores close," Bryant explained.

"Yeah, you need to exchange those gift cards for some real presents," Taylor jibed.

Felicia returned and placed a plate with a waffle on it and a plate with scrambled eggs, link sausage, and hash browns in front of Bryant, who was sitting at the other end of the table.

"Did I hear you say you're going shopping?" she asked as she sat back down at the head of the table.

"Yes ma'am'," he responded and started eating.

"I can go with you if you want a little help," she said.

"I'm just running in and out a couple of stores," he tried to dissuade her from going with him. "I'll be all right."

"Well, you can take my car," she said then smiled as she watched him devour his breakfast.

It was almost noon when Bryant backed his mother's silver Infiniti out the driveway and headed toward the Northwood Shopping Plaza, about three miles away. Bryant didn't care too much for shopping, which is why he started giving gift cards instead of presents. If he had to go shopping when he lived in Chicago, he preferred it be at the Northwood Shopping Plaza. The apartment he lived in before he moved to Atlanta was a few blocks from the plaza, so he was familiar with the plaza and its stores. He hoped he would have time after he finished shopping to ride by and look at the apartment, where he lived for three years.

The road had been plowed, but ice and snow were starting to accumulate again. So, he took his time driving through the neighborhood to the main highway. The radio was playing Nat King Cole's "The Christmas Song," his mother's favorite holiday song. That was followed by another one of her favorite holiday songs, "Silent Night," by the Temptations.

Bryant turned on the highway and headed south. He figured the icy conditions would keep people at home and off the roads, but that wasn't the case. There was more traffic on the highway than he expected, and the traffic was moving faster than he wanted to drive. He was glad he only had to drive about two miles on the highway before turning off on Malloy Street, a two-lane street leading to the shopping plaza. As he approached the intersection of Malloy and Porters streets, the drivers in front of him began to tap on their brakes until they came to a complete stop. Bryant leaned forward to see what was causing the backup. He was seven cars back from the intersection, but it looked like there had been a collision in the middle of the intersection. He looked in his rearview mirror. Several cars were behind him, so he couldn't back up. The cement barrier between the lanes prevented him from turning around. He knew it was going to be a while before the accident was cleared, so he eased out of the traffic lane and pulled into the parking lot of a beauty supply store and hair salon that were closed for the holidays. He decided to walk down to the intersection to see what happened, so he put on his black wool beanie and his gloves before getting out the car.

A Toyota Corolla, a Cadillac Escalade, and a Land Rover were involved in the crash. The front bumper was hanging off the Corolla. It appeared to Bryant, at least, that the Corolla caused the accident. He looked around to see if anyone had been hurt. The driver of the Escalade, a middle-age man, was standing beside his vehicle and talking on his cell phone. A mother and her two young teens were in the Land Rover when the accident occurred. They stood huddled together on the sidewalk as bystanders checked to see if they were okay. He glanced around for the driver of the Corolla but didn't see anyone standing around looking like they had been in an accident. Then the door of the Corolla opened, and a young woman stepped out the car. The driver of the Escalade rushed over to her and asked if she was okay. She didn't respond. Her eyes filled with tears as she started walking toward the café on the corner of the intersection. She didn't appear to be hurt physically, but she was visibly shaken. She opened the café's door, went inside, and sat down in a booth by the window.

From across the street, Bryant watched her gaze out the window past the vehicles in the middle of the intersection, past the policemen and tow truck drivers arriving on the scene, past him and the other bystanders at something or someone no one else could see.

Chapter 4

Opening her own café was something Pearlie Mae Simmons had dreamed about since she began washing dishes and then cooking at the Dew Drop Inn when she was thirteen. She started working at the Dew Drop Inn, a small café that used to be on the southside of Chicago, in 1962, and she worked there until the café closed in 1976. She worked at a couple of other restaurants, until 1982, when her husband, Jake, an automotive mechanic, opened his own garage, and she left the kitchen to manage the garage's office. The garage was prosperous, and they lived a good life. But she never gave up on her dream of opening her own café. In 1993, she and Jake were taking a Sunday evening drive when they saw a "For Sale" sign in the window of the old Malloy Street Grill. They stared at the sign. Neither said a word. Neither had to. Jake took his time driving through the intersection then pulled to the curb and stopped in front of the cafe. Four months later, Pearlie Mae's Café opened its door.

The café sat on the corner of Malloy and Porters streets. The large windows surrounding the café offered drivers and pedestrians passing through the intersection an unobstructed view inside. Bryant had driven by the café almost daily when he lived in the apartment near the shopping plaza, but he never stopped to go inside. He did, however, accept the invitation to look inside when he drove by. If the stoplight stopped him, he had about thirty seconds to watch the happenings inside the café. When the light was green, he drove slowly through the intersection so he could at least glance inside. Diners sat in booths by the window, at a row of tables on both sides of the café, and at the L-shaped counter. He kept telling himself he was going to stop one day and go inside. He wanted to sit at the counter, order the day's menu special, then enjoy his meal while staring back at the people passing outside the café. But he never did.

The snow had stopped falling.

As Bryant stood across the street from the café staring at the young woman sitting alone in the booth by the window, he felt the urge to go inside. He wasn't interested in sitting at the counter and ordering from the menu today. He wanted to go inside so he could talk to her and make sure she was okay. She looked so alone, and it wasn't because she was the only one sitting in the booth. Bryant was still pondering whether he should go inside the café and talk to her when he realized he had crossed the street and was standing in front of the café. The door opened and a man walked out with a carryout bag in his hand. The man said excuse me because Bryant was blocking the walkway. Bryant apologized then moved to let the man out. He caught the door before it closed. Then, after taking a deep breath to calm his nerves, he stepped inside Pearlie Mae's Café for the first time.

"Welcome to Pearlie Mae's," said Mabel, the older of the two waitresses. "Will you be dining in or placing a carryout order?"

"I just want to check on her," he said, nodding toward the young woman in the window booth. She was still staring blankly out the window.

"Let me know if you need anything," Mabel said and walked into the kitchen.

Bryant took off his beanie and gloves and put them in his pocket as he walked to the booth. He stood there for a few seconds before saying anything, but she didn't seem to notice.

"May I have a seat?" he asked.

She didn't respond.

Bryant sat across from her. "My name's Bryant," he said. "And, I just want to make sure you're okay."

She continued to gaze out the window.

"Is there someone I can call for you?" he asked.

He expected her to remain silent and continue acting like he wasn't sitting across from her. But she didn't.

"He's out of town," she said, without looking away from whatever she was staring at.

"Who's out of town?" Bryant asked.

"My fiancé," she answered.

An awkward silence followed.

Bryant looked out the window and saw two police officers talking to the man who drove the Escalade and to the woman driving the Land Rover. The man driving the Escalade pointed at the Corolla and then toward the café. The officer turned and started walking toward the café. Jake Simmons, who looked ten years younger than his seventy years, saw the police officer coming toward the café, and walked out the kitchen, from behind the counter and greeted the officer at the door.

"I think he wants to talk to you about the accident," Bryant told the young woman. "Would you like for me to…"

"No," she answered before he could finish asking. "I'm okay."

She stood and walked over to the officer.

"Hi, I'm Officer Stephens," he introduced himself. "Are you the driver of the Toyota Corolla?"

"Yes, I am," she responded.

"First, are you hurt or injured?"

"No," she replied. "I'm fine."

"Well, I need you to walk out here to the car with me, so I can take a look at your license and registration," the officer explained.

"Okay," she said. "They're in the car." Then, she turned and glanced at Bryant, who was still sitting in the booth by the window.

Bryant saw her look over at him, which prompted him to say, "I'll wait here for you."

The officer held the door open for her, and she walked out in front of him.

Bryant watched as she opened the car door, took her registration papers out the glove compartment, then handed the papers to the officer. Her driver's license was in her wallet, which was in her purse. She gave him the license. She grabbed her phone off the seat.

A woman eating a bowl of chili and crackers at the counter asked Jake for change to play the jukebox in the back corner of the café. Jake gave the woman the change, then walked over to the booth where Bryant sat. "I'm glad no one was hurt," Jake said as he looked out at the intersection. The Escalade and the Land Rover were already on the curb, and the tow truck was backing into position to pick up the Corolla.

An old Johnny Taylor song, "Play Something Pretty," began playing on the jukebox.

"This was one of my wife Pearlie Mae's favorite songs," Jake said. His head rocked back and forth.

The young woman's eyes stayed on the cafe like her gaze could keep Bryant there.

"Is she a friend or a relative?" Jake asked.

"I just met her," Bryant answered. "I saw she had been in an accident, and I came over to make sure she was okay.

The door opened and a young couple entered the café.

"Well, she looks like she could use a friend," Jake said. "Especially, with it being Christmas." Then, he walked over to the counter and greeted the couple, who, after noticing the mistletoe hanging above the door, were locked in a kiss.

Chapter 5

The door opened, and she walked back in.

Bryant was waiting where he said he would be. He didn't hear her when she stepped up to the booth and said, "I'm Cassie." He was too distracted by the spark and then glimmer surfacing in her eyes. Her timid smile. Her fingers brushing curls of hair behind her ear distracted him too. He was still gazing at her hair, dark auburn with lightly brushed highlights that perfectly complemented her caramel-brown skin tone, when she asked, "Did you hear me?"

He didn't hear her, but he saw her lips moving. So, he asked, "What was that?"

"I'm Cassie," she responded.

"Hi Cassie," he replied. "I'm Bryant."

Cassie stood at the booth, waiting for Bryant to offer her a seat. When he didn't, she asked, "May I sit down?"

"Of course," Bryant answered. "Have a seat."

She took off her cinch-waisted gray parka and laid it in the seat across from Bryant. She was wearing a pair of fitted black jeans, a black sweater, and a pair of gray boots. She sat down and placed her Hobo leather handbag on the seat beside her.

"I'm sorry about the accident and your car," he said.

"It was my fault," she admitted.

"It could've been the road conditions," he suggested an alternate explanation for the crash. "It's snowing and there's ice on the road."

But she placed the blame squarely on her. "I wasn't paying attention," she said and looked out at the traffic flowing steadily through the intersection. "My fiancé called as I was approaching the intersection and said he wouldn't be home for Christmas. The next thing I know, I was driving through a red light and plowing into two vehicles."

Bryant watched her gaze out the window. Before he could figure out what to say, she spoke.

"He's in Memphis," she said. "We moved here from Memphis eight months ago when his job transferred him here. He's a logistics regional manager, so he occasionally flies back down to Memphis to coordinate projects. He was supposed to be back today, but something..." Her voice trailed off.

"It's probably the weather," Bryant speculated. "I was supposed to fly from Atlanta to Chicago today, but a snowstorm was forecasted to hit Atlanta this morning, so I flew in yesterday."

"The weather?" she considered. "I hadn't thought of that."

Bryant detected the sense of relief in her voice. He wished he had not. Now, he couldn't help but wonder what other reason her fiancé would have for being hundreds of miles away from her on Christmas Eve.

He was relieved when Jake walked up to the booth and asked if they needed anything. Bryant ordered a cup of coffee, black, and Cassie ordered a cup of hot chocolate. Jake walked over to the counter, and a minute later, returned with the coffee and hot chocolate. "By the way, I'm Jake," he said. "Pearlie Mae was my wife."

"I'm Cassie."

"Bryant."

"It's a pleasure to meet both of you," Jake said. "If you need anything, just wave for me."

As soon as Jake walked behind the counter to his seat at the cash register, Shirley, the younger waitress, walked out the kitchen putting on her coat. "I'll see you tomorrow, Uncle Jake," she said and hugged Jake. Then, she waved to the six customers in the café and wished them all a "Merry Christmas" as she walked out the door.

Bryant glanced down at his watch. It was almost two o'clock.

Cassie was sipping on her hot chocolate when her cell phone rang inside her purse. "It's probably him calling back," she said. She took the cell phone out her purse.

Bryant, wanted to give her some privacy, so he told her was going to the restroom. As he walked toward the restroom, he glanced over his shoulder and saw her answer the phone.

When he came out the restroom, he saw that she was still on the phone, so he stopped and surveyed the song chart on the old model jukebox that still played records. Nearly all the records were rhythm and blues hits from the sixties, seventies, and eighties. There were a handful of songs from the nineties, and they were all by artists from the previous decades. He was reaching in his pocket for change when he noticed she was not on the phone. He took his hand out of his pocket and walked back over to the booth.

"So, you're from Chicago, but you live in Atlanta," she said as soon as he sat down. "How long have you lived in Atlanta?"

"Two years."

"What do you do?"

"I'm a newspaper reporter," he answered.

"Sports?" she asked.

"No. I write mostly news and features. Some investigative reporting."

"Do you like it?"

"Love it, would be a better description," he answered. "Your turn now. You're from Memphis but you've been living in Chicago for seven..."

"Eight," she corrected him.

"Eight months," he continued. "Your fiancé works as a logistics manager. What does his lovely…" Bryant shook his head and apologized, "I didn't mean to say that."

"It's okay." Her verbal assurance was followed with a good-natured smile. "I'm a registered nurse. And before you ask if I like being a nurse, the answer is yes. I would work for free, if I already had a million dollars."

"Wow! I like my job, but I don't think I'd do it for free even if I had a million. Do you work in a doctor's office or a hospital?"

"At a hospital. I'm a surgical nurse."

He sipped his coffee and tried to envision her in surgical scrubs.

"My turn," she declared. "Are you married, in a relationship, or single?"

"I'm not wearing a ring, so…"

She countered before he could finish, "Maybe you took it off."

"Good point. Well, the answer is I'm not married. I'm not in a relationship. So, that makes me single."

He wasn't expecting her response or her change in tone. "Why?"

He could tell she was asking a question she really wanted an answer to, but not necessarily from him. "What do you mean, why?" he replied.

"Why are you single? Are you afraid of settling down? Is being single too much fun?"

"I guess I'm waiting for the right woman," he revealed.

"How will you know when she's the right one?"

He answered the best he could. "I'll just know."

Bryant looked at his watch. It was after two, and the stores would be closing at five.

"Do you have to be somewhere?" she asked. "You keep looking at your watch."

"I need to do some Christmas shopping before the stores close."

"You're cutting it close." She checked the time on her cell phone. "I mean really close."

"Actually, I finished my Christmas shopping in Atlanta," he explained. "But when I got here yesterday, my brother told me everyone disliked the gift cards I gave them last Christmas."

"And you bought gift cards this year?"

"Yes," he confessed. "And I need to exchange them before the stores close."

"Wow! I can't believe you bought everyone on your shopping list gift cards."

"I hate shopping, especially shopping for other people, so gift cards make sense. A person gets to choose something they really want instead of having to pretend they like what I picked out. I assume you've been done with your Christmas shopping."

"I put up my Christmas tree the day after Thanksgiving, and I finished all my shopping the next day."

"Well, I better go before it gets too late." He drank the last swallow of his coffee then asked, "Do you need a ride somewhere before I go?"

"No," she answered. "I'll call a Lyft driver when I'm ready."

"All right," he said then stood. "It's been a pleasure, Cassie."

He regretted having to leave her, but he couldn't give his family gift cards for Christmas presents again. He was walking away when she asked, "Do you have some identification?"

He turned around. "Who, me?"

"Yes, you," she said. "If you have identification that you can show Mr. Jake, I'm going to ask if I can go shopping with you. Of course, we'll have to take the bus or call a Lyft driver to take us where we're going."

"I'm going right up the street to Northwood Plaza, and I have my car," he said.

"I don't get in cars with strangers," she responded.

"So, you know every Lyft or taxi…"

She cut him off, "They've been vetted by the company."

"You got me there." Bryant took his wallet out of his pocket and handed Jake his driver's license. He spotted the *Chicago Defender* news rack at the end of the counter. He pulled out his cell phone, went to the phone's photo gallery, and opened a photo of him accepting a media award while standing in front of a *Chicago Defender* banner. "And look here. I was a reporter for the *Chicago Defender*." He handed Jake the phone.

Jake inspected the license and picture on the phone. "He's okay," he told Cassie. He handed Bryant his license and phone and told him, "I want you to remember where you met this young lady. Pearlie Mae's Cafe. That's my wife's name on this café. I don't have to tell you what that means, do I?"

"No sir," Bryant answered.

Cassie put on her parka as Bryant paid for their drinks. He took the beanie and gloves out his coat pocket and put them on.

Mabel looked out the window and saw the bus at a stop down the street. "That bus goes straight to Northwood, but if you plan on catching it, you better get outside. Or, you can take your time and catch the train a street over. It goes to Northwood too."

"Let's take the train," Cassie said. "I've been wanting to ride the train since I got here."

"Okay. We'll take the train."

Bryant opened the door and Cassie stepped back. "You go first," she directed him. "I'm not getting under that mistletoe with you."

"As handsome as he is," Mabel said, "I can't say that I blame you. Might have me doing something I ain't got no business doing."

Jake nudged Mabel. "You need to sit your behind down somewhere," he said. "He's young enough to be your grandson."

"But he ain't," she responded with a sly wink. "Y'all have a Merry Christmas."

Bryant walked out the café and Cassie followed.

The bus slowed as it approached the stop in front of the café, passing Bryant and Cassie as they walked to the corner then turned right and headed for the train station on St. Jeans Avenue.

It was snowing again.

Chapter 6

The doors opened, and she stepped on the train. She sat in a window seat. Bryant sat next to her. Neither moved once they were seated. They sat perfectly still, frozen in place, to keep space between them. A deliberate space. Only a few inches. Just enough of a barrier to keep them in their proper places. After the train pulled out of the station and before it slowed as it approached the next stop on Glendale Street, Bryant felt the space between them began to diminish. She felt it too.

The two middle-age women sitting in the seats across from Bryant and Cassie could tell they were struggling to keep space between them.

The young man who got on the train at the Glendale Street stop noticed the uneasiness between them as he passed going to his seat.

The bus driver who was catching the train home saw it too. When he glanced over at them, he could see how hard they were laboring to keep some space, physical and otherwise, between them.

A connection was budding, and they both knew it was causing the space to shrink and the barrier to give way. There was an awkward silence between them that lasted until the train neared the intersection of Malloy Street and Buford Highway. Snow and ice on a section of the tracks caused the train to wobble. Cassie ended up pressed against the side of the train and Bryant pressed against her. Since there was no space between them to worry about anymore, they were finally able to talk without wondering what would happen if one of them accidentally touched the other.

At least eight years, he told her. That's how long it had been since he rode one of Chicago's famous street trains. He couldn't remember exactly when he took his last ride, but it had to be before he bought his first car, a Chevy Impala, eight years ago. He was a full-time college student working almost full-time as a website copywriter for a marketing company when his mother co-signed with him on an auto loan application. "I used to ride the train all the time when I was growing, especially when I was in college," he said. "I was going to school full-time and working nearly full-time during my senior year, which meant I stayed on the train going back and forth between home, school, and work. That's when I decided it was time to get a vehicle. My train-riding days were over after that."

She told him it was her first Christmas away from home. She was planning to go home to Memphis for Christmas, but she and her fiancé, Malcolm, decided to spend Christmas in their new home in Chicago. Then, she said, Malcolm had to go to Memphis for work and was having a hard time getting back, so she was feeling alone in a big city where she hardly knew anyone. "That's why I asked if I could tag along," she tried to justify her presence. He told her that it was supposed to be his first Christmas away from home until a colleague asked to switch holiday work schedules.

Earlier at the café, she explained how the accident happened. She was on the phone with Malcolm, when he said he was stuck in Memphis and couldn't make it back for Christmas. She was stunned and didn't see the stoplight was on red. On the train, she revealed what happened after the accident and why. "Malcolm heard me scream," she said. "He heard me scream and he heard the sound of my car crashing into two vehicles. All I could hear was him shouting through the phone – yelling my name and asking if I could hear him. I heard him, but all I could think about was being alone in Chicago for Christmas and the reason I was going to be alone. Instead of answering him, I turned off the phone's speaker, got out the car, walked in Pearlie Mae's Café, and sat down. I needed to get as far away as possible from the accident and Malcolm's voice without leaving the scene."

When the train pulled into the shopping plaza and stopped, he held her gloved hand and told her to watch her step as they got off.

There were only a few shopping hours left.

Macy's was their first stop.

Every cash register in the store was open, but that didn't stop the checkout lines from wrapping around each other. Holiday music played throughout the store, but it did little to ease the anxiety caused by last-minute shopping on Christmas Eve.

Bryant was glad Cassie came along to help him exchange the gift cards he bought in Atlanta for real presents for his family. If she had not been there, he may have turned around when he walked in Macy's and saw shoppers racing to beat the clock and store employees wishing the clock ticked a little faster. He knew Macy's was one of his mother and two sisters' favorite stores, so he had gotten them all Macy's gift cards like he done last year.

The store was busier than most days with shoppers rushing to find the remaining items on their Christmas list or scrambling to find gifts for people they forgot to put on their list. Cassie could spot the difference between the two types.

"The lady in the black leather coat," Cassie pointed out to Bryant. "She hates shopping just as much as you, and she waited until the last minute to start. That's why she's about to get every man on her Christmas list a sweater."

Bryant looked at the lady, who was browsing through a display of men sweaters. There were solid colored sweaters – rust, beige, gray, white, and black, and there were sweaters that blended two colors – a different color stripe around the chest and sleeves. There were pullovers and cardigans.

"Watch her," Cassie said. "It's about to be a one-for-all."

Bryant was surprised at Cassie's intuition when the lady picked out a solid rust, gray, and black pullover sweater, two blended colored pullover sweaters, and black and gray cardigan.

"You're talking, but I think that's smart shopping. I bought my brother and brother-in-law preloaded Visa debit cards. I might as well use the cards and get them a couple of sweaters."

"Normally, I would insist you put more thought into it, but the stores will be closing soon, and we've still got to get presents for your mom, sisters, and nephew," Cassie said.

They walked over to the sweater display.

"Don't just grab any sweaters," Cassie instructed him. "Think about it this way. If your brother and brother-in-law were shopping for sweaters, which ones would they choose."

"My brother-in-law is a family man," Bryant thought out loud. "He's laid back, but he's cool. He would pick…" Bryant picked up a solid gray and a solid black pullover.

Cassie looked at the scarves hanging on a rack behind them. She took a gray and black scarf off the rack and handed it to Bryant. He smiled, pleased with his choice.

"Taylor's a senior in college," Bryant thought out loud. "He's cool, hip, a combination of street and Perry Ellis. So, he would pick…" Bryant picked up a solid rust pullover and a black cardigan.

Cassie took a solid black scarf from the rack and handed it to Bryant. "Mark your brother and brother-in-law off your list. Now, for your nephew, mom and sisters." Cassie grabbed Bryant by the hand and pulled him behind her onto the escalator.

"Where are we going?" Bryant asked.

"Upstairs," she answered. "To the home and household department."

"Okay, I get it," Bryant responded. "My younger sister just moved in her own apartment, so I should get something for the apartment."

"Have you been to the apartment?"

"No," he answered. "I was planning to go by later this evening."

"Then not really," Cassie replied. "If this is her first apartment, I'm sure little sister has already hooked it up just like she wants it. And, you'd be shooting in the dark since you haven't seen the apartment."

"That makes sense," he said. "So, what are we looking for?"

"Something for your nephew," she answered, just as the escalator neared the second floor. "His first Christmas gift from his uncle will not be a plastic card."

Cassie reached for his free hand and guided him off the escalator behind her. She left him when he stopped to adjust the four sweaters and two scarves in his arms. By the time Bryant caught up with her in the nursery section, she'd already picked out two walkers for him to choose between. He watched her eyes gravitate toward the more colorful walker, so he chose that one. "That one's my first choice too," she said.

Cassie looked around the store and saw an empty shopping cart in the hallway leading to the restroom. She rushed over to the cart and was pushing it away when the person who left it there walked out the restroom.

"Hey, who moved my cart?" the man yelled.

Cassie ducked behind a row of baby cribs so the man wouldn't see her. Bryant watched as the man looked around for the cart.

"He almost caught me," Cassie said as she pushed the cart up to Bryant.

"Yeah," Bryant said and laughed. "I was praying, Lord please don't let this woman have me fighting over a shopping cart in Macy's on Christmas Eve."

"You were going to help me?"

"Hell yeah," Bryant declared. "What kind of man would I be to stand here and watch you duke it out with another guy?"

"So, chivalry isn't dead."

"No, it's not."

Bryant handed Cassie the sweaters and scarves. He put the box containing the walker in the shopping cart, and Cassie placed the sweaters and scarves on top of the box. Before Bryant could ask where they were headed next, Cassie was already halfway to the elevator.

"Come on," she yelled back to Bryant. "We only have forty-five minutes left before the store closes."

Cassie pressed the button for the elevator.

Bryant watched her as he pushed the cart. The smile on her face, the joy in her eyes, the gleefulness made her even more beautiful than she had been at the café. He thought about meeting her at the café. Christmas shopping with a stunning woman he didn't know three hours ago and feeling a mesmeric attraction he'd never felt. Her standing in the elevator, holding the doors, yelling for him to hurry. The improbability of it all had to mean he was living a dream. He closed his eyes and tried to force them to stay shut.

"I'm just thinking out loud," Cassie said. "But shouldn't you open your eyes so you can see where you're going?"

"The lights." Bryant opened his eyes and placed the blame on the lights. "They nearly blinded me."

"Really?" Cassie asked. "I was thinking the lights were a little dim."

Bryant pushed the shopping cart in the elevator, and Cassie moved her hand so the door could close.

"If we had more time, we'd get gifts that were more personal for your mom and sisters, but since we don't, we're going to get them something a girl can always use," Cassie said as the elevator descended to the first floor.

"You have to be talking about cosmetics and perfume."

"You guessed it." The doors opened and they stepped off the elevator.

Bryant followed her closely with the shopping cart as she browsed through the cosmetics department. She was no longer in a hurry. Instead, she took her time examining the various displays of perfume gift sets. Bryant wished they had the rest of the day and night to shop, but he knew the store would be closing shortly. She was standing at the counter talking to a clerk when he leaned close to her and whispered, "We better choose what we're going to get. The clock's ticking."

She turned and showed him a Carolina Herrera Good Girl Eau de Parfum Gift Set. "I love this," she said. "And I'm sure your sisters would love it too."

"Then, I'll take two of the gift sets," he told the sale clerk.

"No, he won't," Cassie interjected. "You can't give your sisters the same perfume as Christmas gifts."

"You're right again," he replied.

Cassie walked off to examine another perfume display at the end of the counter. When he was sure she wouldn't hear him, he told the clerk to give him two of the Good Girl gift sets anyway.

Bryant was using the gift cards to pay for the perfume gift sets and the other items when the manager announced over the intercom that the store was closing in fifteen minutes and urged shoppers to make their way to the checkout areas. Bryant turned to Cassie, who was reading a text message on her phone, and said, "We made it."

Cassie looked up from her phone and replied, "And we did it with fifteen minutes to spare."

He smiled victoriously.

Chapter 7

The landing. It's on every falling person's mind.

If the fall is precipitated by an intentional step, jump, or dive from the edge, the landing is viewed as a payoff of sorts – a sought after, yet sometimes tragic, reward. But, if the fall comes after a misstep, slip, stumble, or even a push, the landing – what waits at the end of the fall, is what the falling person fears most.

Bryant knew he was about to fall, which meant if he fell, it wouldn't be because of a misstep, slip, stumble, or push. He knew he was standing at the edge when he saw a reflection of the two of them in a glass pane on their way out the store and he thought they looked like a happy couple. He felt himself wanting her and wanting to be hers even though he knew she already had a fiancé. Still, he didn't have to fall. He could have let her get in the Lyft driver's Kia Sorento by herself and he could've call for another driver. Instead, he chose to step off the edge knowing the landing – how it all ended, could be tragic.

As Bryant placed his shopping bags and the box with the walker in the backseat of the Sorento, he watched Cassie get in on the other side. She reached for the bags and box and pulled them in the middle of the seat so he would have room to get in. As she put the box on the floor, she pretended not to notice him staring at her.

"Do you have enough room?" she asked.

"Yes," he responded.

"If you don't," the Lyft driver said, "You can put the bags back in the rear."

"That's okay," Bryant answered as he got in and closed the door.

The driver pulled away from the curb and started out the parking lot. "You're going to Malloy and Porters street, and then to…"

Cassie cut the driver off. "Yes," she said. "He's getting dropped off on Malloy and then you can drop me off."

The driver turned out the parking lot onto the highway.

"I'm glad you came with me," Bryant told her.

"Thanks for letting me come," she replied. "If you hadn't, I would be at the apartment sitting around by myself, wishing I was back home in Memphis."

The hour and a half they spent racing around Macy's was the best time he'd ever had shopping, and Bryant wasn't ready for his time with her to end. He stared out the window and wished he could increase the drive time to his mother's car. In a few minutes, ten at the most because of the icy roads, the Sorento was going to pull up to his mother's car, he was going to get out with his shopping bags and box, put them in his mother's car, then turn around just in time to yell "bye" before the Sorento drove away. Since she was going to be home alone, and because he wanted to see her again, he contemplated inviting her to his mother's house for Christmas dinner. He was trying to figure out a way to invite her when his cell phone rang.

It was Taylor calling.

"Man, where are you?" Taylor asked as soon as Bryant answered the phone.

"I'm leaving the shopping center," Bryant responded in a tone just louder than a whisper. "What's up?"

"Everybody's here but you," Taylor informed him. "Mom just asked about you, and Talia was about to call you, but I told her I would."

"I should be there in a little bit," Bryant said. He covered the phone and told Cassie, "It's Taylor." Bryant put the phone back to his ear.

"Why are you whispering?" Taylor asked. "And covering the phone to keep me from hearing?"

"I'm not whispering."

"Yes, you are." Cassie mocked his whispering. "Can you even hear yourself?"

"Who was that?" Taylor asked.

"That was the radio," Bryant answered.

"No, it wasn't." Cassie leaned toward Bryant and said into the phone, "I'm Cassie."

"Put me on speaker," Taylor yelled in the phone. "Bryant!"

"Turn on the speaker," Cassie urged.

Bryant reluctantly turned on the speaker.

"Hi Taylor," Cassie said.

"What's up?" Taylor greeted her. "Have we met?"

"No," she answered. "I just met your brother today."

"Really?"

"Really," she answered.

"May I ask where and how?"

"You can ask me when I get home," Bryant jumped in. "Is there anything else?"

"No," Taylor answered. "Like I said, I was calling because everybody's here and Mom asked about you."

"Well, I'll be there in…" Bryant managed to say before Taylor cut him off.

"Before you hang up, take me off the speaker." Then, before Bryant could turn off the speaker, Taylor asked, "What does Cassie look like? Is she bad?"

Bryant looked at Cassie.

"Answer him," she said.

"She's beautiful," Bryant told Taylor.

Cassie blushed. Bryant thought she was even more beautiful when she blushed.

"Yes really," Bryant spoke into the phone.

"What did he say?" Cassie asked Bryant.

Bryant covered the phone and said, "He doesn't believe me."

Cassie grinned and asked, "Why? Is it because of all the pretty girlfriends you've taken home before?"

Bryant put the phone back to his ear and told Taylor, "I'll talk to you when I get home." Then he hung up the phone.

Cassie looked at Bryant and smiled. "Let me hold your phone."

Bryant handed her the phone. "What are you going to do?"

"We're going to take a selfie and send it to your brother," she answered.

"For real?"

Sensing Bryant's uneasiness, she asked him, "What's wrong? You said I was beautiful, didn't you?"

"And you are. I'm just a little camera shy."

"What's your password?" she asked.

"I don't have one."

"I don't believe this," she said as she turned on the phone's camera. "A guy who doesn't have a password on his phone."

"That's because I don't have anything in my phone to hide."

Cassie stopped and stared at Bryant. "Nothing?" she asked.

"Nothing."

She smiled and said, "Lean this way, so I can get a good shot."

Bryant placed the shopping bags on the floor and leaned over closer to her.

"Let me know when you're ready," she said.

"I'm ready."

"Then smile and say Merry Christmas." He did and she took the picture.

"I hope it came out okay," Bryant said as he leaned over to look at the picture.

"It did." She handed Bryant the phone. "Now, send it to Taylor."

Bryant sent the picture to Taylor in a text message.

Almost instantly, Taylor texted back, *Wow!*

The Sorento slowed as it approached the stoplight at the intersection of Malloy and Porters Street. The light changed from yellow to red, and the driver stopped.

Bryant and Cassie both gazed out the window at Pearlie Mae's Café. They could see Jake and Mabel talking to two customers seated at the counter. Two other customers were seated in a booth by the window.

The light changed to green, and the driver turned on Malloy Street. Bryant's demeanor turned solemn as he thought about saying goodbye to her. He wasn't ready. By the time the Sorento turned in the parking lot and stopped next to his mother's car, Bryant had figured out how to spend a few more minutes with her, how to keep the moment going a little longer.

"The café's still open," he said as he got out the Sorento. "Would you like to get a bite to eat before you go? My treat."

"Since you're treating, yes," she answered then opened the door and got out.

Bryant put the shopping bags and box in his mother's car. While she was talking to the driver, he took one of the Good Girl perfume gift sets out the bag and eased it inside his pocket. As they walked up the sidewalk toward the café, the streetlights came on and lit the way.

Chapter 8

The city was shutting down for Christmas. Most of the businesses along Malloy Street were already closed. The ones that hadn't closed their doors before the streetlights came on were turning the keys and locking up. Except for Pearlie Mae's Café.

Jake was coming out the kitchen when Bryant and Cassie walked in the café.

"Look who's back," Jake said, announcing their entrance. "Did you find everything on your shopping list?"

"I did," Bryant answered. "Thanks to this expert shopper."

"Well, I wouldn't call me an expert, but..." Cassie thought about what she was saying. "But I am."

Mabel walked out the kitchen with her coat on and her pocketbook in her hand. "I will see you good folks the next time," she said.

"You're not getting ready to close, are you?" Cassie asked Jake.

"No," he answered. "We're open until eight o'clock."

"It would be open until midnight if it was left up to him," Mabel added. "I'm leaving early so I can get home and start my Christmas dinner. My son, his wife, and four children are coming for dinner tomorrow. But mark my word, they're going to show up in time for breakfast."

Mabel looked out the window and saw her husband's car pull up to the curb.

"There's the husband, so I better get going," Mabel said and started toward the door. "Merry Christmas."

"Merry Christmas," they all responded.

Mabel opened the door and stopped under the mistletoe. "Willie!" She knew he could not hear her because the car windows were up. "Willie! You don't see this mistletoe?"

"You better hope he doesn't," Jake advised and tried not to laugh. "If he does, he might take off, and you'd have to catch the bus home."

Bryant covered his mouth with his hand to keep from laughing. And, Cassie tried not to laugh when she said, "Mr. Jake, that was mean!"

Mabel laughed too. "It was mean, but true," she told Cassie. "If Willie thought I was calling him to come kiss me under the mistletoe, he'd tell me what they used to tell 'em in Wadie's Bar."

Jake grinned and said, "They're too young to know anything about Wadie's."

"They may be, but I betcha they can guess what they told you in Wadie's when you got 'em wrong," Mabel countered. She looked at Cassie and asked, "What do you think they told 'em?"

"Where to go?"

"Go straight to hell." Then she looked at Bryant and asked, "What else they used to tell 'em?"

"What to kiss?"

"And I mean kiss their black..." Mabel started.

Before she could finish, Jake yelled, "You better not. This ain't Wadie's!"

Mabel laughed out loud. "If they didn't tell you where to go or what to kiss, they told you about your mammy."

Willie blew the car horn.

"Mabel, I ain't taking you home," Jake warned.

"Let me go before this man leave me." Mabel heeded Jake's warning. "Y'all good folks have a Merry Christmas." The door closed behind her. She waved as she got in the car, and they waved back.

~~~~~

Bryant and Cassie sat in the same booth.

Since Jake was working by himself, and because neither of them was hungry, they both ordered a slice of red velvet cake and a cup of coffee. After Jake brought the cake and coffee over to the booth, he went back to the counter and rang up the bill for the silver-haired couple who had been sitting two booths behind them. "I hope you all have a Merry Christmas," Jake said and gave them their change.

"We wish the same for you, Jake," the husband said. "We're going to try to make it on home before this weather gets any worse."

On their way out the door, the woman looked over at Bryant and Cassie and wished them "Merry Christmas."

"Merry Christmas," they responded.

When the door closed behind the couple, Jake picked up an empty cleaning tray and walked over to the table where the Jenkins were sitting. As he passed Bryant and Cassie's booth, Cassie asked, "Do they have far to go?"

"No," Jake answered. "That's Mr. and Mrs. Jenkins. They live two buildings down from here. They been coming here two, three times a week since Pearlie Mae first opened the door."

Bryant looked at Cassie then reached inside his coat. "I have something for you,"

"For me?"

"It's just a token of my appreciation for all your help today. Trust me. I couldn't have done it without you."

"You didn't have to get me anything."

"I wanted to," he said and handed her the Good Girl perfume gift set she liked so much. "You said you loved it."

"I do," she told him. "I just can't believe you slipped behind my back and got two anyway."

"I didn't get a chance to smell it in the store," he said. "You mind?"

She opened the gift set and took out a bottle of the perfume. She sprayed a light stream in the air then waved her hand in the stream. She extended her hand. "What do you think?"

The smile obscuring his face answered her question.

Jake put the cleaning tray behind the counter. He asked as he walked over to the jukebox, "Y'all don't mind if I play a little music, do you?"

"No sir." Bryant turned around in his seat, so he could see Jake. "I noticed your jukebox had a lot of oldie-goldies on it."

"Nothing but oldie-goldies," he told him. "And they're all Pearlie Mae's favorites. Over the years, she picked every record on here." He laughed. "She used to have the hardest time when a new record came out that she liked, which meant she had to take something off to put it on. It would take ole girl a couple of days to decide what to take off because she loved them all. And, I love every song on here because she did." Jake put eight quarters in the jukebox. "Anything in particular you want to hear?"

"I love old school music, so whatever you play is fine," Cassie replied.

"Same here,' Bryant said.

"It's Christmas, so let's start with my girl Darlene." Jake pressed the code for the record then jokingly pleaded, "Pearlie Mae, won't you please come home!" When the song came on, he began to finger pop and sing along, as he pressed codes for other songs.

"This is one of my favorite Christmas songs," Bryant said then began singing along. Cassie was smiling, but there was no joy in her smile, no sign of happiness in her eyes. Bryant stopped singing and asked, "What's wrong?" Before she could answer, he realized how the song related to her situation. "Hey, I'm sorry. I wasn't thinking."

"That's okay," she said. "He'll be here in a couple of hours."

"But I thought…"

"He texted me while you were in the checkout line," she explained. "His flight was re-routed, so he'll be home tonight."

Bryant wanted to be happy for her. He was glad she didn't have to spend Christmas alone, but he wanted to be the one spending Christmas with her.

"I should have told you earlier," she said. "I'm sorry."

He saw how his displeasure was tainting what should've been a joyful moment for her, so he painted on a smile and told her, "Don't be. Your fiancé's coming home. Now, you can spend your first Christmas away from home together."

Cassie stared out the window. The stoplight changed, but there were no cars stopped or driving through the intersection. "He said he couldn't leave me home by myself on Christmas, especially after the accident."

"And he shouldn't. But why am I sensing you're not really happy about it?"

"I guess I can tell you this since I'll probably never see you again after tonight," she turned to him and said. "I wished Malcolm looked at me the way you do."

"I can't help it," Bryant responded before he thought about what he was saying. "No one's ever made me feel like I'm feeling right now."

Cassie didn't want to ask, but she needed to know, "How do you feel?"

"Like I've met the girl I've been waiting for since fifth grade."

Cassie felt a chill coursing through her body as she moved closer and closer to the edge. When Bryant first walked in the café after the accident, he sat down across from her, and made her feel like she was the only woman in the world just by looking at her. She tried her best to ignore how he made her feel, but now, she felt herself slipping over the edge, falling for him. To slow her descent and ease her landing, she reached for her safety net – telling him and reminding her heart, "Malcolm and I are getting married this spring."

Chapter 9

Cassie and Bryant were stuck, unable to move past the moment she reminded herself and told him she was marrying Malcolm in the spring. He said something like, "That's great," but it was a mechanical, knee-jerk response, not a real indication of what he was thinking. After that, they just sat there, unaware time didn't stop just because they couldn't find a way to move forward.

While they were contemplating how not to ruin the incredible day they'd had, Jake shut down the kitchen. He wiped down the counter. Hummed, finger popped, and swayed to four songs. Adjusted the jukebox so it would play without additional quarters. Then punched the codes for a few more songs. There was only one song, Marilyn McCoo and Billy Davis Jr.'s "You Don't Have to be a Star," left to play.

"I don't mean to rush you young folks, but I'll be closing up in about fifteen minutes," Jake announced, as he finished tallying the register receipts.

"I guess it's that time," Cassie said. She took out her cell phone and ordered a ride through the Lyft app.

"I can drive you home," Bryant told her.

"Thanks, but that's okay," she responded. "I've kept you away from home long enough already. I'm sure your family's wondering where you're at. Wait. Your brother's probably told them where you were."

"And with who, as soon as he hung up the phone." Bryant finally looked up at her. "He's shown them your picture and they're probably all sitting in the living room staring at the front door, hoping you walk in with me."

"So, they're expecting me?" she asked.

"I said hoping, not expecting," he clarified.

Cassie looked directly into Bryant's eyes and confessed, "I would love to, but I can't."

"I know," Bryant acknowledged and stared back into her telling brown eyes. "Will you make me a promise?"

"It depends on what you're about to ask me."

"I hope your marriage works out," he said. "I really do. I want you to have a wonderful marriage and a happy life. But, if for whatever reason, it doesn't work..."

"Why wouldn't it work?" she inquired as though he might already know.

"Because he doesn't look at you the way I do."

Cassie felt him drawing her in, looking deep inside her and feeling what she was feeling. She closed her eyes to keep him away from her heart.

"Promise me that you'll find me if it doesn't work out."

"Find you?" she asked.

"You won't have to look far," he told her. "I'll be right here on Christmas Eve waiting for you."

"You're going to be here next Christmas Eve?"

"Every year, every Christmas. Waiting for you."

Cassie nodded disbelievingly. "What if our marriage works and Malcolm and I live happily ever after?"

"Then I'll become a Christmas Eve fixture at the café."

"Do you know how crazy that sounds?"

"Yes, it's crazy," he admitted. "But, like I said, I've been waiting for you since fifth grade."

Jake dimmed the lights on the backside of the café as the last song ended.

"I'll say it for you, Mr. Jake." Cassie seized the opportunity to change the subject. "We don't have to go home, but we gotta leave here!"

"That's what time it is." Jake walked in the kitchen and returned putting his coat on.

Cassie looked outside and saw a silver Honda stop in front of the café. "My Lyft driver's right on time."

Bryant stood first. He reached for her hand and helped her out the booth. She thanked him.

"It was a pleasure meeting both of you," Jake said as they walked toward the door.

"Likewise," Bryant responded and opened the door for Cassie. "Thanks for putting up with us."

She stopped and told Jake, "Have a Merry Christmas."

Jake answered, "You too, Sweetie."

Cassie noticed Bryant staring at her. "What?" she asked.

He looked up at the mistletoe hanging above the door and then at her.

"Go ahead," Jake urged. "It's just a Christmas kiss."

Cassie's eyes gave Bryant permission to lean in close and kiss her, softly, but not to touch her soul like he did. She fought the temptation to throw her arms around him, and he held onto the inside of his coat pockets to make sure his arms stayed put.

They waved bye to Jake as the café's door closed behind them. They walked over to the Honda, and Bryant opened the back passenger-side door for her.

"Cassie." He stopped her before she got in the car. "I didn't get your last name."

"I know." Tears formed in Cassie's eyes as she got in the car. "Thank you for being there today."

"I'm glad I was here," he replied. "And I'll be here at Pearlie Mae's next Christmas Eve waiting for you."

"If it doesn't work."

"I'll be here." Bryant saw the tears flowing from her eyes as the car pulled away from the curb. He choked back his own tears as he crossed the street. Halfway across the street, he felt compelled to look back, to turn and watch the car she was in disappear in the distance. He barely noticed the car horn blowing for him to get out the street.

Chapter 10

Bryant was turning in his mother's driveway before he realized he had made it to the house. Kyle's blue Equinox was parked on the curb in front of the house, and Taylor's car and Talia's red Focus were in the driveway. Bryant parked behind the Mustang. He turned off the car then sat staring at the picture of him and Cassie on his phone. Even with the picture as proof, he was having a hard time believing everything that had transpired – from meeting her to shopping with her to kissing her underneath the mistletoe.

Everyone was at his mother's house, but they weren't all sitting in the living room waiting for him to walk in like he told Cassie they would be. Samantha was in the kitchen helping her mother peel and cut potatoes for potato salad. They got started in the kitchen around four o'clock, so they were well into preparing their Christmas dinner. They had already baked two cakes – a coconut cake and a carrot cake. A sour cream pound cake was in the oven. The collard greens were picked, cut, washed, and ready to be cooked. So were the green beans. Sweet potatoes for pies were boiling in a pot on the stove. The ham was in a pan ready to go in the roaster. And the turkey was thawed and ready for Kyle, Bryant, and Taylor – it took all three, to inject it with creole seasonings and drop it in the turkey fryer. In the morning, while the men tackled frying the turkey outside, Samantha and Felicia were going to cook the collard greens and green beans, roast the ham, bake the sweet potato pies, and mix the potato salad.

Talia rarely helped in the kitchen, and tonight was no exception. She was in the living room trying to teach her seven-month-old nephew, Kyle Jr., how to say what she felt should be his first words, Auntie. Talia was also responsible for the evening's music – Christmas tunes she played on her cell phone. The music played in the background just loud enough to be heard when no one was speaking.

Kyle and Taylor were in the den playing a game of basketball on the PlayStation. Taylor's team was winning by a large margin, but the momentum shifted, and Kyle's team charged ahead. When Kyle's team was behind, Taylor couldn't get a word out of his brother-in-law. So, he slacked up and let Kyle's team come back. Kyle started bragging once his team took the lead, which made the game more exciting. When Kyle and Samantha arrived at the house, Kyle was tired and exhausted after working five straight twelve-hour days. Winning the game and two Heinekens had reinvigorated him. Taylor played well enough to stay within two or three points, but he never took the lead back. Seeing the smile on Samantha's face when she walked in the den after hearing her husband laughing and talking smack made losing deliberately worth it for Taylor.

Taylor glanced at his cell phone. It was 8:47. He knew Bryant was hanging out with Cassie, but he expected him to be home before everyone left. Samantha and Kyle were going to be heading home soon so they could put Kyle Jr. to bed. Talia was going home because she and Jennifer were cooking a Christmas dinner at their new apartment, and he was going over there for dinner after eating dinner at home. Taylor couldn't wait any longer. He picked up the phone and dialed Bryant's number.

Bryant had just made up his mind to get out the car when his phone rang, and the call screen replaced the selfie with Cassie. It was Taylor calling. "I'm outside in the driveway," Bryant answered the phone. "I'll be right in."

"Good," Taylor replied. "Man, I thought I was going to have to put out an APB on you."

Bryant heard Kyle in the background ask, "Where is he?"

"He just pulled in the driveway," Taylor told him.

"Is she with him?"

"I don't think so," Taylor said.

Bryant hung up the phone and got out the car. Since everyone was inside, he decided to leave the gifts in the car and slip back out later and get them.

Talia was waiting for him when he opened the living room door. "So, where have you been all day? Everybody's sitting here waiting on you. I'm waiting. Mom's waiting. Taylor's waiting. Samantha and Kyle's waiting. And you know Kyle Jr.'s been waiting seven months to meet his uncle. But I heard you forgot all about us to run off with some girl you met at the mall."

"I didn't meet her at the mall." He took off his beanie, gloves, and jacket.

"So, where did you meet her?"

"Hold on before you answer that," Samantha yelled as she and their mother hurried from the kitchen to the living room.

Bryant walked over to Talia and reached for Kyle Jr. "Hey K.J. I'm Uncle Bryant." Bryant took Kyle Jr. in his arms then sat on the sofa. "I think he looks like me."

"They think that too." Talia sat beside Bryant. "But I think he looks like me."

Their mother sat on the loveseat and Samantha sat next to Bryant so she could play with Kyle Jr.

"So, where did you meet her?" Samantha asked.

"Wait!" Taylor yelled as he and Kyle raced into the room. "I still have first listening rights." Taylor sat in the recliner and Kyle sat on the loveseat beside his mother-in-law. Taylor shifted back and forth until he got comfortable. "Okay. Tell me about this dream girl."

"I didn't say she was a dream girl."

"You said she was beautiful with her sitting right beside you," Taylor refuted. "Men don't say things like that to a woman's face unless he's lying or she's a dream girl. We saw the picture, so we know you're not lying."

"What Taylor said," Kyle concurred.

"She is pretty," Talia added. "But…"

"She's beautiful!" Samantha placed her hand on Bryant's hand and asked, "How did you and Cassie meet?"

"How do you know her name?"

"Taylor told us."

Bryant looked at Taylor and Taylor offered an explanation. "She yelled her name in the phone. Remember?"

"Anyway, I was driving up Malloy on my way to Northwood Plaza. When I got near the intersection of Malloy and Porters – Pearlie Mae's Café' is on the corner…"

"I've eaten there a couple of times," Taylor interrupted Bryant. "As a matter of fact…"

"Will you hush?" Talia cut him off. "He's trying to tell us how they met."

"My bad," Taylor apologized then sat back in the recliner.

"There was a wreck at the intersection, so traffic had stopped and was backing up in every direction. I got out the car and walked up to the intersection to see what had happened. She had run the red light while talking on her phone and hit a Land Rover and an Escalade. She was sitting in her car under the stoplight. The other drivers were standing outside their vehicles waiting for the police to get there, but she just sat in her car. Then all of a sudden, she got out the car, didn't say a word to anyone, and walked in the café and sat in a booth by the window."

"Was she in shock?" his mother asked.

"She said she just needed to step away from it all," he explained.

"So, how did you actually meet her?" Talia inquired.

"I walked over to the café and sat down in the booth where she was sitting," Bryant explained.

"You mean, you just walked up and sat down with this woman you never met?" Taylor shook his head disbelievingly and sat up in the recliner. "When did my big brother start mackin'?"

Bryant laughed. "Is that what it's called?"

Samantha's curiosity peaked. "What did you say?"

"Well, before I sat down, I asked her if it was okay. She didn't respond, so I sat down. I introduced myself, asked her if she was okay, and the conversation started from there."

Talia turned off the music on her cell phone then pulled up the picture of Bryant and Cassie. "This wasn't taken in Mom's car," she said and made sure everyone saw the picture.

"We caught a Lyft ride from Northwood Plaza."

"Why?" Samantha asked. "You had Mom's car."

Bryant was about to explain when Kyle intervened. "You don't have to answer my wife's question."

Kyle looked at Samantha, who turned around so she could look him in his face and ask, "What do you mean he doesn't have to answer my question?"

"Because you are too deep in the man's business," Kyle responded. "You're his sister. Not his mother."

"You're right," Samantha admitted. "Mom, ask Bryant why for me!"

Felicia laughed. "I think I'm going to have to agree with Kyle."

"I was just about to tell Talia's nosey behind the same thing," Taylor said. "Get out the man's business!"

"I know the person who forwarded the picture to everyone in here isn't talking," Talia shot back.

"That's spreading his business, not getting in it," Taylor countered.

"Tomayto, tomahto," Talia quipped.

Bryant looked over at his mother. He could never hide what he was feeling from her. She was looking at and within him. She saw past the painted-on smile and the put-on grin and felt his loss. She knew he'd met and had a wonderful time with a beautiful woman who could've stepped out of his dream. She also knew the dream was slipping away from him and there was nothing he could do to stop it. "The fellows are right," she said and smiled at Bryant. "Leave him alone."

"I will after he tells me this," Talia continued. "When do you plan on seeing her again?"

Bryant handed Kyle Jr. to Samantha then stood and walked toward the stairway.

"Bryant," Talia called. "Did I say something wrong?"

He stopped at the bottom of the stairway. "She has a fiancé and they're getting married in the spring," he divulged then walked up the stairs to his bedroom.

Chapter 11

Cassie lay on the sofa staring blankly at the glistening lights on the Christmas tree in the corner by the front window. In an hour, the sun was going to rise on their first Christmas in their first apartment. Malcolm was still asleep, and she figured it would be mid-morning by the time he woke up. He had gotten in after midnight. She was in bed pretending to be sleeping when he came in the room. He tipped-toed, trying not to wake her up. He took a shower then climbed in bed and snuggled up close to her. Five minutes later, he was sleeping like a log. She felt bad about lying next to Malcolm and thinking about Bryant. So, she got up and went and lay on the sofa.

She thought she'd be able to put everything that happened in the back of her mind before she made it to her apartment last night. Her tears had dried by the time she got out the Lyft driver's Honda in front of her apartment, but she was still thinking about Bryant. When she unlocked the door and stepped inside the apartment, she thought about how the space disappeared between them as they sat next to each other on the train. While taking a shower, she thought about him kissing her under the mistletoe at the café. Malcolm called during his flight layover, but she could barely remember what he said because, instead of listening to him, in her mind she was hearing Bryant sing, "Please Come Home For Christmas" as it played on the jukebox in the café. She made a turkey and tomato sandwich that she didn't have the appetite to eat after she remembered staring out the back window of the Honda and seeing him standing in the middle of the street watching the car as it drove away. A new day was dawning, and she was still wiping tears from her eyes and wondering if she'd ever see him again.

As soon as the sun rose, she called her parents, Nathaniel and Margaret, in Memphis and wished them a Merry Christmas. She told her dad how much she missed being home for Christmas and how she thought she was going to be spending Christmas alone. He told her that never would have happened. If push came to shove, he said, he and Margaret would have driven Malcolm back to Chicago even if it meant not getting there until late Christmas Day. Cassie laughed when she thought about Bryant walking toward the elevator in Macy's with his eyes closed. She told her mother she was cooking steaks, baking potatoes, and making a spinach and greens salad and a strawberry cheesecake for their Christmas dinner. She asked her mom did they like the Christmas presents Malcolm stopped by the house and dropped off while he was in Memphis. Her mom told her they decided not to open presents on Christmas Eve because Darryl – Cassie's only sibling – wasn't going to make it in until around nine o'clock because of the weather. Before hanging up, Cassie's mom asked her was there anything else she wanted to tell her. Cassie said no and wondered aloud why she asked. Her mom heard her. "I just sense something's weighing heavily on you," she responded. "I hear it in your voice and feel it in your spirit. You didn't get hurt in the accident yesterday, did you?"

"No ma'am," Cassie answered. "The accident and worrying whether Malcolm would make it back or not, had me a little on edge, but I'm okay now."

"Are you sure?"

"Yes ma'am."

After the call, Cassie was glad she didn't tell her mother about Bryant. Her mother would've had a fit if she told her she had met Mister Right and he's not Malcolm after they've mailed her and Malcolm's engagement announcements to more than a hundred relatives and friends.

Taylor and Kyle loved the sweaters and scarves.

Kyle and Savannah loved Kyle Jr.'s walker.

Savannah and their mother loved the perfume gift sets.

And Talia loved the Good Girl perfume set.

"Spray a little on," Bryant urged Talia after she unwrapped the gift. She sprayed a light mist on her wrist. Bryant closed his eyes and inhaled deeply. The perfume's sweet floral fragrance reminded him of Cassie.

"Did you pick this out?" Talia asked. "I'm willing to bet she did, and that it's one of her favorites. That's why you're sitting here about to suck up all the air."

"Talia, when you're right, you're right," Taylor chimed in. "I bet she's the reason we didn't all get gift cards again this year."

"She helped me pick out your gifts," Bryant confessed, "but I was on my way to exchange the gift cards when I met her."

"I knew you had bought gift cards," Taylor said as he tried on the cardigan sweater. "That's why I told you what they said about last year's gift cards when I picked you up at the airport."

"Taylor, you didn't!" Felicia rolled her eyes at Taylor.

"I had to," Taylor declared. "What was I supposed to do? Leave my brother in the dark and let y'all talk about his gift cards again?"

"They? Y'all?" Talia snapped. "How about we? You're the one who first brought it up."

"That's because I knew what y'all were thinking," Taylor shot back.

"Hold up," Kyle jumped in. "I didn't say one word."

"Samantha said it for you," Taylor enlightened him.

"Boy, don't you make me..." Samantha stopped midsentence. She shook her head and grinned. "Not now Samantha. It's Christmas."

After exchanging and opening Christmas presents, Samantha and Felicia headed to the kitchen to finish their part of the Christmas dinner, and Bryant, Kyle and Taylor got ready to fry the turkey. Talia picked up Kyle and got out the others way.

Taylor and Kyle set up the fryer and heated the oil, while Bryant was inside injecting the turkey with the creole seasonings. Taylor and Kyle had been waiting to get Bryant away from the women so they could ask more specific questions about Cassie. But, as soon as Taylor brought up her name, Bryant said he didn't want to talk about her anymore. He told them she was someone he met and had a great time with, but it was over because she had a fiancé and they were getting married in the spring. That's what he said, but it's not what he was feeling. He wished he could see and talk to her right then, but he knew she was spending Christmas with the man she was going to marry. He tried not to think about her, but every other breath he found himself wondering what she was doing with him. He imagined they were sitting on the floor unwrapping Christmas gifts. She handed him the five presents she had gotten him. When he opened the first present, his eyes lit up. She'd picked out the perfect gift for him. He leaned over and kissed her. Bryant rubbed his eyes and shook his head to erase the picture of him kissing her.

"Man, I've been around you with some of the women you've dated, but I've never seen you this bothered by one," Taylor said. "I mean, you only spent a few hours with Cassie, and now you're moping around and acting all heartbroken."

"Heartbroken?" Bryant laughed. "Man, go on with that craziness."

"I don't know, brother-in-law," Kyle said as he checked the turkey. "You got that look in your eyes."

"What look?"

"Like you fell for her," Kyle answered.

"And now you're missing her," Taylor added.

"How?" Bryant questioned. "We met and spent a few hours talking and shopping. Now, I'm supposed to be crazy in love?"

"Did you kiss her?" Kyle asked.

"What?"

"You heard him," Taylor responded. "Did you kiss her?"

"What does that have to do with...?"

"Answer the question," Taylor demanded. "Did you kiss her?"

Bryant hesitated before saying, "Yes. As we were leaving the café, I kissed her under the mistletoe hanging over the door."

Taylor looked at Kyle then they both turned, looked at Bryant, and yelled, "You fell!"

Later, when they sat down for dinner, Bryant took his usual place at the head of the table in his father's seat. He expected someone to mention Cassie, but no one did. He assumed Kyle and Taylor told the others what he had said about not wanting to talk about Cassie, so no one brought her name up during dinner or the rest of the day. That evening, Bryant's plan was to go with Taylor to Talia's apartment for a late Christmas dinner. He got dressed to go but changed his mind while walking down the stairs behind Taylor.

"You know what," he stopped and said midway down the stairs. "You go ahead. I'm a little tired and don't really feel up to it."

"Are you for real?"

"Yeah, it's been a long day."

"Talia's going to be pissed," Taylor replied.

"I know," Bryant said. "I'm going to call her, and I'll stop by to see the apartment before I leave tomorrow."

Bryant turned and went back to his room. He heard Taylor tell their mother he was leaving. When she asked where Bryant was, Taylor told her he changed his mind about going. She said she was going upstairs and talk to him, but Taylor told her he was fine and just needed to rest. Bryant silently thanked Taylor then closed the bedroom door.

Chapter 12

Bryant was glad to see the dawn. It was the day after Christmas, and he was flying back to Atlanta. He'd only gotten a few hours of sleep, having spent most of the night tossing and turning – thinking and trying not to think about her. He got out of bed a couple of times, sat by the window, and stared out at the night. He was sitting at the window when Taylor pulled in the driveway. He stepped away from the window so Taylor wouldn't see him. Then, he climbed back in bed and pretended to be sleep in case Taylor decided to check in on him.

A few minutes after sunrise, Bryant tip-toed out the room and downstairs. He thought everyone would be asleep, but when he walked in the kitchen, his mother was pouring a pot of water in the coffeemaker. "Good morning," she said. "Coffee will be ready in a few minutes."

"Good morning," Bryant said and kissed her on the jaw. "Why are you up so early?"

"I was about to ask you the same thing."

Bryant sat on a stool.

"You couldn't sleep?" she asked as she took two coffee cups from the cabinet.

"I get up around this time for work, and my internal clock doesn't seem to know I'm on vacation."

"I know what you're talking about. I've been retired six months, but I wake up every morning the same time I used to when I was working." She took two saucers out the cabinet and a knife and two forks out the drawer. She sat them next to the three cake dishes on the counter. "So, how was your Christmas?"

"It was nice," he answered.

"Just nice?" she probed.

Bryant didn't respond.

She cut two slices of the pound cake and placed them on the saucers. "We don't have any business eating this pound cake for breakfast, but if you don't tell, I won't." She poured two cups of coffee then handed Bryant one of the cups of coffee and a slice of cake.

As he nibbled on the cake and sipped the coffee, Bryant struggled with how to tell his mother what he was still having a hard time telling himself. She knew Bryant wanted to tell her something, but instead of asking she sat there eating her cake and sipping her coffee. Finally, Bryant blurted out, "I think she was the one, Mom. I know you don't believe in love at first sight. I don't believe in it either. At least, I didn't until I met Cassie."

"You said she 'was' the one."

"That's because our paths crossed too late. She's getting married."

"So, what are you going to do?"

He was just about to tell his mother what he told Cassie as they were parting when they heard Taylor come down the stairs yelling, "I don't smell anything cooking!"

Felicia changed the subject before Taylor walked in the kitchen. "Didn't you say you have to work tomorrow?"

"Yes ma'am. That's why I'm flying back this afternoon."

Taylor walked in the kitchen and saw what they were eating. "I'm going back to bed," he said. "Wake me up when you put some pots on the stove."

It was 11:14 when Bryant and Taylor pulled out the driveway in Taylor's black Mustang. Bryant's flight was at 4:40, but he wanted to stop by Talia's apartment before Taylor dropped him off at the airport. He kissed his mother goodbye and told her he would see her in May when he came home for Taylor and Talia's graduation.

She claimed she was coming to Atlanta to visit him before then. Taylor suggested she wait and go to Atlanta with him for his last collegiate spring break. She said she would think about it.

Talia was looking out the window of her apartment when Taylor's Mustang pulled in the parking lot. She greeted them at the door. Jennifer was standing behind her. Talia gave Bryant a tour of the two-floor apartment, while Taylor helped Jennifer move something in her bedroom. As Talia and Bryant were coming back downstairs, she told him, "I forgive you about last night."

"I'm sorry I couldn't make it, but I was…"

Talia cut him off. "No need to explain."

After eating lunch – leftovers from Talia and Jennifer's Christmas dinner, Bryant and Taylor left for the airport.

"I need you to drive by the café on the way to the airport," Bryant told Taylor when they got in the car.

"What café?"

"Pearlie Mae's on Malloy."

Taylor didn't ask why. He didn't need to.

As they approached the stoplight at the corner of Malloy and Porters – the intersection where he first saw Cassie, Bryant told Taylor what he was about to tell his mom earlier that morning. "I told her I would be here next Christmas Eve," he disclosed.

"Be where?"

"At Pearlie Mae's."

The light turned red and the Mustang stopped at the intersection.

"Why? I thought you said she was getting married."

"She is," Bryant stated and stared across the street at the café. "I told her I will be here Christmas Eve waiting for her in case the marriage didn't work."

Taylor searched for the right words and right way to respond. Finally, giving up, he said, "Man, you know what? I'm going to leave that one alone. I'm going to let you be crazy all by yourself."

Bryant whispered to himself, "I'll be here."

~~~~~

As much as she loved Christmas, Cassie was glad it was over. After being off from work for the past three days, she couldn't wait to clock in the next morning and get back to caring for patients. Malcolm, who was off too, woke up late and decided he wanted seafood for lunch, so they were in his car on their way to his favorite seafood restaurant, which wasn't far from Pearlie Mae's Café. Cassie knew he was going to want to ride by the intersection where she had the accident, and sure enough, when he saw the Malloy Street sign, he turned on the street and headed toward the intersection. Earlier that morning, she woke up and decided to put Bryant out her mind after thinking about him constantly during the past two days. Riding by the place where they met and where he said he would be waiting for her wasn't helping her forget him.

As they approached the intersection of Malloy and Porters Street – Pearlie Mae's Café sat on the corner, the stoplight turned red. Cassie looked ahead at the intersection. There were two cars in front of them. A woman driving a silver Acura was right in front of them, and two black guys in a black Mustang were at the light.

"Is this the intersection?" Malcolm asked.

"Yes," she answered.

"Were you coming from this direction?"

"Yes." She could see inside the café. She saw Jake walk out the back and stand at the counter. She smiled.

The light turned green. Cassie watched as the black Mustang drove through the intersection and then the silver Acura. As Malcolm drove through the intersection, she gazed at the empty booth where they sat in the café. She whispered to herself, "He'll be here."

Next Year

Chapter 13

Time was winding down. Bryant wouldn't have known this if not for the hands circumventing the square-faced clock on the wall in the living room. He'd been sitting on the sofa thinking about Cassie and staring blankly into space since coming in from work around 5:30. He wasn't sure how long he'd been sitting there, until he noticed the hands on the clock had moved. The shorter hand was now pointing at nine instead of a little past five, and the long hand was pointing straight up instead of straight down.

Since returning to Atlanta from Chicago, Bryant had not been able to get back into the swing of things. He moped through the day, and then daydreamed wistfully through the night. John, Cal, and nearly everyone in the newsroom could tell that Bryant wasn't himself. After two days of seeing the despondent cloud encircling Bryant, John and Cal decided to take him to lunch at Olive Garden so they could find out what was bothering him. "How was Christmas in Chicago?" John asked Bryant after the server walked away.

"It was nice," he answered. "I had a great time with the family. I got to meet my nephew, and I hung out one night with Taylor and Talia."

"And?" Cal pushed for more.

"What do you mean, and?"

"And what else happened? It doesn't take a psychic to know something happened while you were in Chicago."

"For real," John added. "It's written all over you."

Bryant took a deep breath before revealing, "I met someone."

"I knew it!" Cal blurted. "You're lovesick. That's why you've been moping around."

"I wouldn't call it that," Bryant responded.

"Then what would you call it?"

"Let's just say, I met the one, and..." Bryant thought about the moment he saw Cassie get out her car, walk in the café, and sit in the booth by the window. "Her name's Cassie."

Bryant told them how he was going shopping to get his family gifts instead of the gift cards he'd gotten them when he met Cassie at Pearlie Mae's Café after she'd had an accident in the intersection under the stoplight. He told them about the two of them shopping for presents for his family, returning to the café, and kissing under the mistletoe.

The server walked up to the table with their order. As soon as she placed Bryant's plate in front of him, he began eating. She had placed John and Cal's plate in front of them and walked away, when Bryant looked up and saw John and Cal staring at him.

"You kissed her under the mistletoe, then what?" John asked.

"The Lyft driver was waiting, so I walked her to the car and opened the door." Bryant took another bite of his chicken parmesan. He took his time chewing, purposely delaying telling them what followed. "This is good," he said.

"Please get on with the story," Cal urged. "Did you see or talk to her later?"

"No," Bryant answered.

"Why not?" John questioned. "It sounds like the two of you had a great time together."

"We did." Bryant closed his eyes and remembered seeing the tears in her eyes as the Lyft driver drove away that night. "Something happened to me that day that's never happened before."

"Don't say it!" Cal shook his head.

"He's going to," John predicted it. "I hear it coming."

Bryant admitted, "I fell in love."

"I can't believe you said it!" Cal grinned. "Let me get my condolences ready."

John sensed the seriousness in Bryant's admission. He asked, "If you fell in love, why didn't you call or see her again?"

That's when Bryant told them what he deliberately left out earlier. "She has a fiancé, and they're getting married in the spring."

It wasn't what John and Cal expected to hear, so both had to gather their thoughts before responding. They heard Bryant's story and understood how he could fall in love with a beautiful, smart, and captivating woman like he described Cassie as being. But he had left an important part of the story out – a major plot twist that would've no doubt made them ask how he could let himself fall in love knowing all along she had a fiancé. Before either could figure out what to say, Bryant uttered something else neither John nor Cal could begin to grasp.

"I told her I would be at the café waiting for her on Christmas Eve in case she doesn't get married or the marriage doesn't work," he disclosed and waited for their reactions.

The perplexed look on their faces told him what they could not fix their mouths to say.

It was New Year's Eve, so the reporting staff that wasn't covering one of the celebrations around town, left early. Right before Bryant left the office, Cal walked over and asked if he was doing anything that night, and if not, did he want to go to a New Year's Eve party at a friend's house. Bryant declined the invitation and told Cal he would let him know if he changed his mind. It was 9:08. Bryant was still sitting on the sofa, staring at the clock, and thinking about Cassie when his phone rang. It was Cal calling to see if he had changed his mind about going to the party. At first Bryant said no, but then he figured going to the party would at least clear his head for an hour or two. So, he told Cal to text him the address.

When Bryant pulled up to the house in Buckhead, he texted Cal and told him he was outside. Cal met him at the door. So did Rhena.

Rhena, a Spelman graduate, worked in the city's community relations department. She and Bryant had met two years ago when he stopped by the office to pick up a report that he needed for a story he was writing. They became friends, and it wasn't long before they began dating. The relationship wasn't serious, at least Bryant didn't think it was. He always believed that there was a woman who was perfect for him out there somewhere, and he didn't think Rhena was her. He dated two girls in high school, several young women in college, and a few since then. But none of them were this idealized perfect woman he was waiting for. Cal and John told him most men would think Rhena was perfect or as close to it as humanly possible. She was smart and beautiful. She had a regal elegance, but she was cool, approachable, and loved sports. And, she had sex appeal to spare. The day after Christmas, when Bryant returned from Chicago, she called and asked if he wanted to go to a New Year's Eve party with her. He told her he didn't know his work schedule and would get back to her about it. He never did.

Bryant was about to offer Rhena an explanation when she said, "Don't. I'm just glad you're here." Then she reached for his hand, and he began debating whether he'd made the right decision by coming to the party. He was uncomfortable holding her hand and being close to her while Cassie was on his mind and in his heart. When they got inside, he had a drink and drank it fast, which relieved some of his anxiety. A few drinks later, Bryant loosened up and started mingling with Cal and the twenty or so other guys at the party. As the clock approached midnight, everyone began counting down the last seconds of the old year. That's when Rhena rushed over to Bryant.

"Happy New Year!!!" The group blew paper horns and rang bells before singing, "Auld Lang Syne." They were singing the chorus when Rhena turned and faced Bryant. He knew what the seductive look in her eyes meant. She wanted to get closer to him. To touch and kiss him. Usually, she didn't have to want for too long, not with that look. Things were different now. He was changed. He didn't want her to get any closer. Still, when she kissed him, the three Jell-O shots and four shots of Crown made him kiss her back. An hour later, when the party ended, Rhena drove him home because he'd had a drink too many. He staggered into the bedroom and fell in bed. He was half asleep when he looked up and saw her lying in bed beside him wearing only her panties and bra. She kissed him and began unbuttoning his shirt. He shook his head no, and gently pushed her away. He couldn't go through with it. He apologized to Rhena as he got a pillow and a blanket out the closet, then he walked in the living room and lay down on the sofa.

They called each other and talked a few times after that night, but he always found a reason to be busy whenever she wanted to see him. Before he went home for Christmas and met Cassie, they had a laid-back, congenial relationship. She was fun to be with, and he enjoyed hanging out with her. He regretted lying to Rhena, so he decided to tell her the truth. It was few days after Valentine's Day when he told her about Cassie.

"The reason I've been acting the way I have is because I met someone when I went home for Christmas. Her name is Cassie, and I think I love her."

By the spring – around the time he figured Cassie was getting married, Rhena had stopped calling and answering his calls.

Chapter 14

She was beautiful. Stunning. To die for. But Malcolm didn't see it.

Cassie had been looking forward to attending the New Year's Eve fundraising gala sponsored by Vogue XIII, a charity organization that provided college scholarships to inner-city students. The company Malcolm worked for, Rigoni Transports, was one of the organization's major donors, and Malcolm had been invited to attend as one of one of the company's representatives. Malcolm first mentioned the gala to Cassie back in November, a few days before Thanksgiving, so she was on the lookout for a gown to wear to the gala while she was Christmas shopping. She found a black and blue floral organza ball gown by Eliza J. She kept the gown hidden from Malcolm because she wanted to see the look on his face when he first saw her in it. While he was in the shower, she went into the other bedroom and got dressed. She sat in front of the mirror and did her make-up, brushed her hair, then put on her pearl earrings. She stepped into her black stilettos. She was slipping on her gown when she heard Malcolm turn off the shower. She looked at herself in the mirror. The gown highlighted the curves of her slender body. Then, she hurried to their bedroom. When Malcolm opened the bathroom door, she was standing in the doorway. She didn't expect him to be mesmerized or speechless, but she was hoping for a verbal compliment from him or, at the very least, for him to smile and try to hide it.

"Why are you blocking the doorway?" he asked.

"I was about to knock on the door and tell you to get a move on it," she thought up quickly.

"Well, if you let me get in the room, I can get dressed," he replied.

She stepped to the side, and he walked past her into the bedroom. Cassie moped back to the other bedroom. She picked up the stiletto-shaped bottle of Good Girl perfume and sprayed a light mist. Then, to forget the disappointment she felt when Malcolm walked by her without seeing her, she stared in the mirror and tried to see herself through Bryant's eyes.

At the gala, Malcolm was a different man. He paid attention to her. He complimented her. He leaned over and whispered in her ear, "I love you." Twice. His smile, already bright, was luminous when he looked at her. He glowed as long as people were around to gush about how beautiful a couple they were or how in love they seemed to be or to declare him a lucky man. Cassie played along like she always did, but she wondered how much longer she could love a man who only saw her as a woman who complemented him. It was not the first time she thought this, but unlike the other times, now she knew there was a man out there whose eyes filled with marvel, passion, and divine gratitude at the sight of her. Having met that man a little over a week ago is what led her back to Pearlie Mae's Café the second day of the new year.

Cassie was glad no one was sitting in her and Bryant's booth by the window. As she crossed the street, she could see Mabel at the counter taking an elderly couple's order and a waitress she did not know carrying a tray of food to another window booth where three young men sat.

Mabel was tearing the ticket off the order pad when she looked up and saw Cassie walking toward the door.

Mabel placed the ticket in the window for the cook, Theodis, and asked him, "Will you tell Jake I need him to come out here?" Theodis took the ticket out the window and looked over it as he walked to the back office, where Jake was completing some paperwork.

"Welcome to Pearlie Mae's," Mabel greeted Cassie when she opened the door and stepped inside.

"Hi Mrs. Mabel," Cassie responded and walked up to the counter.

"I'm no good with names, so you're gonna have to…"

Jake cut her off. "Cassie!"

"Hi Mr. Jake."

Jake walked up to the counter and stood beside Mabel. "It's good to see you," he told Cassie. "Mabel and I were talking about you the other day."

"We weren't talking about you," Mabel clarified. "We were just wondering how you and what's his name were doing."

"Bryant," Cassie said.

"That's right. Bryant. I told you I'm no good with names."

"Well, I can't speak for Bryant because I haven't seen him since that day, but I've been doing okay."

"I see you're wearing scrubs," Jake said.

"I'm a registered nurse," she informed him. "And I just finished a twelve-hour shift."

"Baby, you must be exhausted," said Mabel.

"I am," she replied. "I work in out-patient surgery, and today was a busy day."

"Can I get you anything?" Mabel asked.

"I'd love a cup of hot chocolate and a few minutes to exhale."

"Then have a seat, and I'll get you that hot chocolate," Mabel said.

Cassie took her coat off as she walked over to her and Bryant's booth by the window. She put the coat in the seat then sat down. She looked across the table and imagined Bryant was sitting there. "Hi," she whispered.

Mabel walked over to the booth and placed a cup of hot chocolate on the table. "Will that be it?"

"I'd like to get some quarters for the jukebox," Cassie said. She took five dollars out of her pocketbook and handed it to Mabel. "Go ahead and take out for the hot chocolate."

"Okay," Mabel said. "I'll be right back."

When Mabel returned with the change, Cassie went over to the jukebox and put in four quarters. She found the song she was looking for – Marilyn McCoo and Billy Davis Jr.'s "You Don't Have to be a Star," which was the last song the jukebox played before the café closed Christmas Eve. She keyed in the code for the song. When it started playing, she keyed the code in again.

Jake was sitting in the booth waiting for her. "Pearlie Mae loved this song," he said when Cassie sat down. "She played it until the needle wore down the grooves in the record and it wouldn't play. You better believe though, before the day was over, she had the man in here putting a new copy on the jukebox."

"It's a nice song, but I'd never heard it before you played it the other night."

"That's probably because it came out ten, fifteen years before you were born," Jake explained. "Me and my wife got Jake Jr. because of this song, so it had to come out around '76 or '77."

"How many children do you have?"

The light in Jake's eyes dimmed.

"Jake Jr. was our only child," he responded. "We lost him to diabetes when he was twenty-one."

"I'm sorry."

"Enough about me," Jake said to change the subject. "How have you been?"

She hesitated before answering, "I've been doing okay."

"Just okay?"

"There's a lot going on right now, but I'm dealing with it." Cassie sipped her hot chocolate, which had started to cool. "May I tell you something that I can't tell anyone else?"

"I'm listening."

"I think I'm in love with him," she stated.

"Bryant?"

"Yes." She gazed out the window. "Before I met Bryant, no one could have made me believe two strangers could meet and fall in love after spending a few hours together."

"Have you talked to him?"

"Not since we left here," she answered.

"Why don't you call him and…"

She cut him off. "I can't. I have a fiancé, and we're getting married in May."

"That changes things." Jake sat up straight. "You've got yourself a real dilemma."

"What should I do?" she asked.

"I'm not going to pretend I know the answer," Jake replied. "Nobody does, but you."

Cassie was still searching for the answer to her question when she stopped by the café a month later, the day after Valentine's Day. That day, as Mabel was serving a customer in the booth behind her, Cassie told Jake about Bryant's vow to be at the café on Christmas Eve. "If I don't get married or my marriage doesn't work, he said I could find him here waiting for me on Christmas Eve."

Jake looked at her and grinned. "When I say I don't know what to say, I mean I don't know what to say."

"I do," Mabel interjected. "If a man told me that, he wouldn't have to wait for me, because I wouldn't be going nowhere for him to have to wait for me. No, not Mabel."

"We didn't know you were listening," Jake responded.

"I wasn't listening. I just happened to hear."

"Cassie, don't you just happen to hear Mabel," Jake warned. "Make up your own mind."

The next time Cassie dropped by the café was a couple of weeks before her wedding. She walked in the café and sat in the same booth. She was polite, but she was clearly not the Cassie who had opened up to them the last two times she was at the café. She sat in the booth staring out the window, but she wasn't watching traffic passing through the intersection or people walking on the sidewalks. Instead, she was reminiscing and searching for a way to turn the clock back to Christmas Eve. Mabel was off that day, but Jake, Shirley, and another waitress and cook were working. When Shirley took a glass of tea to the table, she sat across from Cassie. Before Shirley could say anything, Cassie informed her, "I won't be stopping by after today."

"Why?" Shirley asked.

"Malcolm and I are getting married in three weeks. And, it feels like I'm cheating when I come here to reminisce and think about Bryant."

Chapter 15

Bryant's flight from Atlanta to Chicago arrived a few minutes after noon. It was the first Friday in May and he had flown home to attend Taylor and Talia's college graduations. When he left Chicago the day after Christmas, he started wondering how he would feel when he returned to Chicago knowing Cassie was there. He was still wondering when he got on the plane in Atlanta. He got his answer when he stepped out of O'Hare International Airport. Everything felt changed. The city. Being home. Him. Nothing felt the way it did before he met Cassie. Because she was there, possibly married, working, and living her life, the city had become a captivating place filled with beauty, passion, and a promise that could change his life.

Now that he was back, it was hard for him to focus on anything except Cassie and the time they spent together last Christmas Eve. While he was in Atlanta, the distance between them mellowed his desire to see and be with her. The distance was gone, and there was nothing to keep his heart at bay. That is why he didn't see Taylor's Mustang parked on the curb or hear the car's horn or Taylor yelling his name. Taylor had to get out the car and walk toward Bryant before Bryant saw him.

His first night there, he hung out at a bar near the university with Talia, Taylor, and Jennifer. Taylor and Jennifer had become a serious couple and seeing them together made him think about him and Cassie riding the train to the shopping plaza. He recalled the moment the space between them disappeared and they began to really connect.

When Talia and Jennifer went to the restroom, Taylor, seeing the faraway look in Bryant's eyes, asked, "Did you ever hear from the woman you met Christmas Eve?"

"Her name's Cassie," Bryant reminded Taylor. "And no, I haven't talked to her. I told you she was supposed to get married this spring."

"Did she?"

"I don't know," Bryant answered. "I haven't seen or spoken to her since that day."

"It's the first weekend of May, and we got a month and a half left of spring," Taylor pointed out. "So, she may not have gotten married yet. Are you still planning to wait for her at the café Christmas Eve?"

"What are you talking about?" As soon as Bryant asked, he remembered telling Taylor about his vow to wait for her on the way to the airport.

"You said you were going to wait for her at the café on Christmas Eve in case she didn't get married or the marriage doesn't work," Taylor reminded him.

"I am," Bryant admitted.

"You think she'll be there?"

"I don't know." Bryant turned up the bottle of beer then sat the empty bottle on the table. "Why are we talking about this now? Christmas is six, seven months away. We should be talking about your big day tomorrow."

"Man, talk about being ready!"

Bryant was glad to see Talia and Jennifer walk up to the table.

The next morning, Bryant drove his mother to the university, where they met up with Samantha, Kyle, and Kyle Jr. in the parking lot of the Bloodworth Center. By the time they located their seats in the ticketed reserve seats, the university's president was finishing his welcome address. The School of Business was one of the first to award degrees, so Talia was part of the first group of graduates to receive their degrees. Forty-five minutes later, Taylor received his degree in computer engineering. Bryant was proud of his brother and sister, and it showed. He had to fight back the tears when his mother hugged him and said, "We did it."

After the graduation ceremony, the family celebrated with relatives and friends at Taste of the Island, a restaurant that served buffet-style Jamaican cuisine. Some brought gifts for the graduates. Deacon Hampton, from the family's church, presented both with engraved crystal plaques on behalf of Ebenezer Baptist Church.

It was a little after three o'clock, when Bryant and his mother pulled out the restaurant's parking lot behind Samantha's car. Bryant took a different route home, driving a mile out the way just so he could drive by Pearlie Mae's Café. He figured Cassie might live in the area near the cafe since she was driving by the café when she had the accident. As he approached the intersection, he slowed down so the light would change to red and he would have to stop. His mother sat quietly in the passenger seat. She knew Bryant had driven out the way to pass by the café, but she did not mention it. Bryant gazed inside the café as he waited for the light to change. He saw Mabel serving a customer at the counter and Jake's niece, Shirley, serving three customers in the booth he and Cassie sat in. He was hoping to see Jake, but the light changed. His eyes stayed fixated on the inside of the café as he drove slowly through the intersection.

That night, while Taylor was at Talia and Jennifer's apartment, Bryant did something he had not done since he met her. He used Taylor's laptop to try to locate information about her. He browsed through the wedding announcements in the local newspapers and other online sites. He used "Cassie" as a keyword along with "Chicago wedding announcements" during his search. There were several potential hits, and he checked them all. None were the Cassie he was looking for. He regretted hearing only what he wanted to hear when he was with her. He knew Cassie said her fiancé's name several times, but he could not recall hearing it. If he remembered his name, he could have used it and her name as keywords, which may have produced better results. Afterwards, he checked his Facebook page. Before he met Cassie, he mostly used social media to distribute articles he had written or news and information that he thought was useful or noteworthy. These still made up the majority of his posts and tweets, but occasionally, he would post or tweet things like photos of him posing with Talia and Taylor at their graduation ceremony. He did not post or tweet every day, but he made sure he checked his social media daily. He didn't know Cassie's last name, but she knew his, and he hoped one day he would check his Facebook page and there would be a friend request from her, or he would see her picture pop up as a new follower on Twitter.

The next day, he told his mother he needed to use her car to meet some former colleagues from the *Chicago Defender* for lunch. After the lunch was over, he drove past the street to his mother's house and over to Malloy Street. When he arrived at the café, he pulled to the curb and parked. He looked inside from the car. Shirley was working with another waitress and a cook he didn't know, but he didn't see Jake or Mabel. For a few seconds, he thought about going inside, but then he changed his mind. He had only briefly met Shirley when he was there Christmas Eve, and he wasn't sure she would remember him or Cassie. So, he pulled away from the curb, turned on Malloy Street, and headed to his mother's house.

He flew back to Atlanta bright and early the next morning.

Chapter 16

There was no turning back.

Cassie knew when her dad, Nathaniel, walked her down the aisle of Mt. Olive Baptist Church and she took her place at the altar next to Malcolm, there would be no turning back. She would become Malcolm's wife, and he would become her husband. They would be one, which meant there would be no place she could hide her feelings for another man. So, before she and Malcolm flew to Memphis the next-to-last weekend of May, she decided to forget Bryant. It did not take long for her to realize forgetting him was like learning to live without breathing.

Their wedding was the last Saturday of May, and she and Malcolm had spent the week of the wedding in Memphis preparing for their big day. Memphis was their hometown, so most of their family and friends were there. Cassie had planned and arranged everything from the week's activities to the wedding and reception with the help of her mother, Margaret, and Malcolm's mother, Priscilla. Cassie's five bridesmaids and maid of honor hosted a luncheon for her the Wednesday before the wedding. Margaret and Priscilla hosted the rehearsal dinner. Before the rehearsal dinner ended, Malcolm's groomsmen whisked him away for a bachelor's party that lasted until dawn. At least that's when Malcolm stumbled into the hotel suite where he and Cassie were staying. She was waiting up for him.

"Where have you been all night?" she asked.

"At my bachelor's party," he answered and kicked off his shoes. He walked in the bedroom, and Cassie followed.

"It's six in the morning!"

"That's why I'm going to bed. We have to be up in a few hours." Malcolm undressed and climbed in bed.

"I want to know where you've been." Cassie stood beside the bed. "What have you been doing, Malcolm?"

"I've been hanging out with my friends." He rolled over in bed and looked up at Cassie. "What do you think I've been doing?"

"Have you been with her?"

"Who is her?"

"You know who I'm talking about."

"Listen Cassie. I don't know how many times I have to tell you this, but I am not seeing Anita, and I haven't seen or talked to her in almost two years."

"We've been together four years."

"Okay, I messed up. I've told you I was sorry and that it would never happen again at least a hundred times. I don't know what else to do to make you believe me."

Tears filled her eyes as she stared down at him. He sounded so convincing, but he sounded that way before the morning she stood in the hallway in front of his apartment and watched him open his door then kiss her goodbye. Malcolm saw the tears in her eyes and sat up in bed.

"I was with your brother until about fifteen minutes ago," he said. "Call and ask him."

He reached for her hand. She took a step back, away from the bed and shook her head no.

"Do you really think I'm so low that I would fool around with another woman the night before our wedding? Do you?"

She wiped the tears from her eyes.

"I love you, Cassie. No one but you."

She took a step closer to the bed. "Just me?"

"Just you."

She placed her hand in his and he guided her into the bed and inside his arms.

Ten hours later, she was ready to become Malcolm's wife. Dressed in a white Vera Wang textured organza wedding dress with a flattering draped bodice and an asymmetrical skirt with a split-front overlay, she looked like an angel standing in the church's foyer waiting to march down the aisle to her future husband. As she watched the flower girl Tiffany, her brother Darryl's four-year-old daughter, start down the aisle, Bryant and all the possible lives she could have with him flashed in front of her. Then she heard the music, "Canon in D" by Pachelbel. It was time. She waved goodbye to the life she could have had with Bryant, then she locked the memories they had already made in the remote recesses of her mind. She took her father's arm, and they stepped inside the church. She glanced down the aisle at Malcolm standing at the altar. He smiled.

"You ready?" her father asked.

"Yes," she said. "Yes, I am."

After taking that first step, Cassie knew there was no turning back. Cassie Diana Knight was about to become Mrs. Cassie Knight Phillips.

Chapter 17

It was the second Tuesday of December, and Bryant was covering a Marietta City Council meeting. As Bryant listened to the council debate whether or not it should approve the proposed budget for a new municipal soccer complex, he filled in the blanks he'd left in the story that he'd written ahead of time. He added quotes from Mayor Tumlin and the city manager as they were spoken. The only thing left to do was to insert the actual vote in the story's second paragraph, since the lead paragraph already stated the council approved the budget.

Bryant looked at the time on his laptop. It was 8:30. He figured the meeting would be over in about thirty minutes, which meant he would still have a couple of hours to hang out at Caesar's Sports Bar with Cal. He was ready for the council to vote so he could email his story to the night news editor, then hurry over to the bar and pig out on a basket of teriyaki wings. He was hungry when he got to the meeting, because he spent his lunchbreak at Macy's searching for a Michael Kors black leather satchel handbag for his mother. He heard her admiring a lady's Michael Kors handbag when he was home for Talia's graduation in May. Bryant knew that even though she loved the handbag, she was way too tight on the purse strings to pay what it cost. So, he decided to get her one for Christmas. Finding the handbag at Macy's, meant he was done with his Christmas shopping. He had gone to the mall the previous weekend and bought presents for everyone but his nephew Kyle. That same night he ordered Kyle's gift online and had it shipped to his mother's house in Chicago.

When Bryant walked in the newsroom after his lunchbreak, Cal asked him what he had for lunch. Bryant told him he skipped lunch to shop for his mother's Christmas gift. If Bryant had told him that a year ago, Cal would have been surprised because he knew how Bryant felt about shopping. But he also knew Bryant was a changed man after he came back from Chicago last Christmas. Bryant told Cal and John, now an editor at the paper, how he met the girl of his dreams on Christmas Eve and showed them the selfie he took with her. He told them about her accident, meeting her in the café, going shopping, and kissing her under the mistletoe. He even told them about her spring wedding and his vow to be at the café every Christmas Eve waiting for her in case the marriage didn't work out. They thought his story was romantic and his feelings for Cassie authentic, but they felt her wedding had already written the story's ending.

After spending a few more minutes discussing the proposed soccer complex, the council voted unanimously to approve its $7.1 million budget. Before Mayor Tumlin could finishing thanking the council for supporting the project, Bryant edited his story's lead paragraph, inserted the unanimous vote in the second paragraph, emailed the story to his editor, shut down the laptop, and was walking up the stairs toward the exit.

Cal was sitting at the counter finishing his second beer when Bryant walked in Caesar's. Bryant had called Cal on his way to the bar and told Cal to order a basket of teriyaki wings. As soon as Bryant sat on the stool next to Cal's, the bartender placed a beer and a basket of wings in front of him. He didn't waste any time getting started.

"Are we going to have that $7 million recreational soccer field?" Cal asked.

"Construction starts in the spring," Bryant answered.

"I guess I better smarten up on my soccer game since Marietta's about to become Soccer City, USA." Cal told the bartender to give him another beer. As Cal reached in his back pocket for his wallet, he glanced over his shoulder and saw Rhena walk in with two other women. He nudged Bryant and said, "Guess who just walked in."

Bryant looked over his shoulder and saw Rhena and her friends walk over to a booth by the window. She saw him looking back at her. He waved and she waved back. He turned around, but he could still see her in the mirror behind the bar's counter.

"I can't believe you just threw her to the curb like you did," Cal said.

"I didn't throw her to the curb," Bryant corrected him. "She's the one who broke it off."

"That's because you told her you were in love with a woman you met and spent a few hours with on Christmas Eve. A woman whose last name you don't even know."

"Who told you that?"

"You!"

Bryant shook his head and told himself, "I've got to stop talking so much."

"You're a reporter, so I don't know why you won't do a little digging and find out who she really is," Cal continued. "That's what I would do."

"Yeah and catch a stalking charge." Bryant had considered doing what Cal suggested numerous times. In his mind, he mapped out research paths that would lead him to her, but he could never go through with it. She deliberately didn't tell him her last name. As they were parting, he mentioned that she hadn't told him her last name and she said she knew. He felt he would be invading her privacy and intruding in her life if he tried to find out any other way.

Bryant finished the last wing and ordered another beer. An hour later, they decided it was time to go. "See you at the j-o-b in the morning," Cal said as they walked toward their cars.

"Talk to you then," Bryant replied.

"By the way." Cal opened the car door. "Since you're not giving gift cards this year, see if you can pull my name in the drawing tomorrow. I already know what I want you to get me."

"Man, get in the car." Bryant got in his Accord.

Cal laughed as he got in the car and closed the door. He backed up then pulled out the parking lot. Bryant pulled out behind him. Twenty minutes later, Bryant sat on the sofa in his living room and stared at the Christmas tree he put up the day after Thanksgiving. It was his third year in the apartment but his first year putting up a Christmas tree. His thoughts drifted back to when he and Cassie were sitting in the booth in Pearlie Mae's after they came from the shopping plaza. He already knew he was falling for her before they made it back to the café. After they got back, and before she told him she was getting married, he realized she was falling too.

He started counting down the days until he would be back at the café where they met.

Chapter 18

Bryant's flight was scheduled to leave Atlanta's Hartsfield-Jackson International Airport at 9:30 the morning before Christmas Eve. Around 4:20 that morning, Bryant pulled in the paid parking lot at Hartsfield-Jackson, took out his suitcase and carryon bag, locked the car, went inside the airport, and asked the ticket agent if an earlier flight was available. He did not expect one to be available. He was at the airport three hours earlier than he needed to be to make sure nothing got in the way of him being on that 9:30 flight to Chicago. He wasn't worried about the weather delaying his flight because it was unseasonably warm in Atlanta and only a light snow was in the forecast for Chicago. What worried him was the possibility of unexpected situations that he would have no control over. He didn't want to be driving to the airport and the car broke down or for an accident to stall traffic for hours. After the ticket agent told him there was nothing available, Bryant found a seat and settled down.

A light snow was falling when his flight arrived in Chicago.

Taylor, Talia, Samantha, and Kyle were all working, so Felicia was tasked with being at the airport when Bryant's flight arrived from Atlanta. She pulled up to the curb just as he was walking out the airport. Bryant put his luggage in the backseat and was about to get in the car, when Felicia got out. "You're driving," she said and walked around to the passenger side of the car. "I hate driving in this airport traffic." She got in the car and Bryant closed the door. He got in then pulled away from the curb into the exit traffic lane.

As he drove, he thought about going to the café the next day. He had no way of knowing how her marriage was going or even if they married in the spring, so he wasn't sure what to expect when he showed up at the café the next day.

"Slow down," Felicia said. "Why are you in such a big hurry?"

Bryant looked at the speedometer. He was driving 70 miles per hour, fifteen miles over the speed limit. "I didn't notice I was driving that fast."

"I can tell," she said. "Is everything okay?"

"Yes ma'am," he answered. "It was a long, hectic week at work, and I'm still trying to shake it off."

When they got to the house, Bryant unpacked and placed his presents under the Christmas tree. The battery-powered car he ordered for Kyle Jr. was still in the box in the basement. Bryant opened the box and made sure all the parts were included. He planned to put the car together later that evening after Taylor made it in. Felicia was gone to the grocery store and Bryant was straightening the leaning Christmas angels on the front lawn when Taylor turned in the driveway and parked.

Bryant was surprised by how grown-up Taylor looked when he got out the car wearing a business suit. "Damn… look at you," Bryant said as he walked toward Taylor.

"What's up big brother?"

"You man," Bryant responded and hugged Taylor. "When did engineers start dressing like boardroom executives?"

"When I became an engineer," Taylor replied and grinned. "I had to present a project concept to a new client, and I just wanted to let them see who they were working with."

"Well, you showed them."

"I did, didn't I?"

After dinner, Taylor sat in the basement watching Bryant put the battery-powered car together for Kyle Jr. Taylor talked about working full-time at the tech firm, designing a new app with two guys he graduated with, his off and on relationship with Jennifer, Talia being accepted to the MBA program at the university, their mother wanting a she shed, and then, finally, the conversation turned to Cassie and the café.

"Are you going to the café tomorrow?" Taylor asked.

"Yes," Bryant answered as he placed the stick-on designs on the car.

"I've been thinking," Taylor said and waited for Bryant to reply. When he didn't, Taylor told him, "When I said, I've been thinking and paused, you were supposed to ask about what."

"About what?"

"If you really want Cassie to be happy and for her marriage to work out like you said you do, then don't you think you're putting a hex on the marriage by going to the café and waiting for her? You wouldn't go if you were really hoping or expecting the marriage to work."

Bryant looked up at Taylor and considered what he'd said.

"I'm not telling you not to go," Taylor clarified. "I'm just saying."

Bryant decided not to respond. What Taylor said made sense, but only to people who believed in hexes. And he didn't.

The next morning, Bryant was dressed and ready to leave for the café when he came down the stairs. Taylor didn't have to work because it was Christmas Eve, so he was still in bed, and their mother was in the kitchen fixing breakfast. She heard someone coming down the stairs and called out, "Taylor. Bryant."

"It's me." Bryant walked in the kitchen. "Smells good."

"I'm almost done," she said.

"I have to be somewhere, so I'm going to miss breakfast." Bryant poured a cup of coffee.

"Where are you going so early?" his mother asked.

"To the café," he told her.

She put the lid on the pot of grits then turned and looked at Bryant. "May I ask why? I'm fixing breakfast."

Unless Taylor had slipped and told someone, he was the only member of the family that knew about Bryant's plan to wait for Cassie at the café on Christmas Eve. Before Bryant left for Atlanta last Christmas, he was about to tell his mother, but Taylor walked in the kitchen. They had spoken at least twice a week on the phone, and he had been home in May, but he never got around to telling her. Now, she was asking, and he couldn't lie. "I met Cassie there on Christmas Eve last year," he said. "And I told her to meet me there today if her marriage didn't work out."

"Did it?"

"I don't know," he responded. "I haven't seen or talked to her since then."

Felicia refilled her coffee cup and warned, "You could be setting yourself up for a big disappointment. What if her marriage is fine and she doesn't show up?"

"Then good for her."

"But what about you?"

"I'll be all right," he tried to assure her and himself. He glanced out the window again.

"Who are you looking for?" his mother asked.

"I called a Lyft driver to take me to the café."

"You can take my car," she said. "Taylor's not working today. If I need to go somewhere, he can take me."

"Are you sure?" he asked.

"Yes, I'm sure."

Bryant took his cell phone out of his pocket and sat on the stool at the counter. "Let me cancel before the driver gets here."

Chapter 19

Bryant was back. A year ago, he told Cassie he would be waiting for her at Pearlie Mae's Café on Christmas Eve. It was Christmas Eve, a year later, and he was standing in front of the café trying to decide if he should go inside. It was the first time he contemplated whether or not he was doing the right thing by coming back. When he got out the car, what Taylor said the night before popped in his head. Maybe Taylor was right, he conceded. Being at the café meant he was hoping she didn't get married and the relationship went kaput or she got married and the marriage soured. He wanted her to be happy, but for her to show up like he hoped, meant she had spent the past year feeling dejected in a broken relationship or marriage. He was about to turn around when a voice inside him asked, "What if she shows up and you're not here?" The answer to that question made him dismiss the doubts and step up to the door.

He didn't see Jake or any of the workers. Two security guards, tired but hungry from working the overnight shift, were eating breakfast at the counter. An elderly couple, whom he thought he'd seen in the café the previous Christmas Eve, ate breakfast in a window booth. The Christmas tree was in the same spot it was in last year and most of the decorations were too. He wondered if the mistletoe was still hanging over the door.

Jake was walking out the kitchen when Bryant opened the door and stepped inside the café. "Welcome to Pearlie Mae's," Jake greeted him. "Will you be dining in or placing a carryout order?"

"How are you, Mr. Jake?" Bryant looked above the door. The mistletoe was still there. He took off his gloves.

A look of recognition crept across Jake's face. "I don't remember your name, but I remember you. You're the guy that was with Cassie last Christmas Eve, right?"

"That would be me. I'm Bryant."

"That's right. Bryant, the newspaper reporter," Jake said.

Bryant and Jake were shaking hands when Mabel walked out the kitchen. Her eyes lit up when she saw Bryant. "Well, if isn't Cassie's friend," she said. "You'll have to excuse me. I'm terrible when it comes to remembering names, but I never forget a face."

"Bryant," Jake reminded her.

"That's right. Bryant!"

"Hey Mrs. Mabel. How are you?"

"I'm doing better than I was yesterday, but not as good as I hope to be doing tomorrow."

One of the security guards raised his coffee cup and asked, "Mrs. Mabel, can I get a refill?"

"You sure can," Mabel answered. "I'll be right back," she told Bryant then went over to wait on her customers.

Jake turned to Bryant and asked, "Have you moved back here or are you home for Christmas?"

"Home for Christmas," Bryant answered. "I'm still in Atlanta."

"You wanna have a seat?"

"Yes sir," Bryant answered. "May I see a menu?" Jake handed him a menu, then Bryant walked over to the booth he and Cassie sat in by the window. He sat down and began looking over the menu.

Mabel was still serving the security guards, so Jake picked up an order pad and walked over to Bryant's booth. Bryant decided on a ham and cheese omelet, toast, a glass of apple juice, and a cup of coffee at the end of the meal. Jake wrote the order on a ticket, handed the order pad to Mabel, then walked in the kitchen. Bryant turned and stared out the window at the intersection. The snow had stopped falling and traffic was flowing smoothly. He didn't know what kind of car Cassie drove, so whenever a car passed and he couldn't see the driver, he wondered if she was behind the wheels and driving by to see if he was there. When Mabel brought his order to the table, he was leaning close to the window trying to see inside a passing car.

"You're going to catch a crook in your neck," she warned him. "Here's your ham and cheese omelet, toast with apple and grape jelly, and your glass of apple juice. Let me know when you're ready for your coffee."

"I will. Thanks."

Bryant took his time eating. He was planning to be at the café most of the day, so he wasn't in a hurry. He was just about done eating when Jake walked out the kitchen and over to the booth where Bryant was sitting. He had a pink greeting card envelope in his hand. Jake sat down. He laid the envelope on the table in front of Bryant.

"What's this?"

"Look inside and see," he said.

Bryant looked at the envelope. It was addressed to Jake, but there was no return address or sender's name. He opened the envelope and saw a picture inside. He took his time taking the picture out the envelope. It was a picture of Cassie on her wedding day. Seeing her in the wedding gown broke his heart. Still, he was captivated by how beautiful she was and could not take his eyes off her.

"Cassie came by a few times after you two were here," Jake divulged. "And she always sat in this booth. When I wasn't busy, I'd come sit with her and we'd talk."

"Did she ever talk about me?"

"She told me you might show up today."

"When was the last time you talked to her?" Bryant continued staring at Cassie's wedding photo.

"A couple of weeks before the wedding." Before Bryant could ask his next question, Jake answered it. "I wanna think she got married in May down in Memphis. She sent me that picture, but she hasn't been back since before the wedding. She told my niece Shirley that coming here to feel close to you would be cheating on her husband."

Mabel took another order from one of the security guards. Then she waved the ticket in the air and told Jake, "You got a to-go order."

"You can keep that picture," Jake told Bryant as he got up from the booth. "I think I was supposed to give it to you anyway."

Bryant was thrilled to know Cassie thought about him after they parted. Coming to the café and sending the wedding photo was proof enough that she felt what he was feeling. He looked at the wedding photo and found himself in a troubling place. He was waiting for her at the café where they met like he said he would, and at the same time, he hoped she was happy and that her marriage was working.

The rest of the morning passed slowly. After finishing his breakfast, Bryant bought a copy of the *Chicago Defender* from the vending machine and spent an hour or so reading it. He checked his email on his phone and then his Facebook page. In between reading the newspaper and browsing on his phone, he exchanged Christmas greetings with the handful of customers as they came and went. And he thought about her. After seeing the wedding photo she sent, being at the café made sense to him. He knew she was wondering if he kept his promise to be at the café waiting for her. It didn't matter where she was, what she was doing, or how close her husband was standing to her, Bryant knew he was on her mind.

It was Christmas Eve, so Jake didn't expect much of a lunch crowd. His niece Shirley came in to work the lunch hour just in case Jake and Mabel got busy. It's a good thing she did. Mabel was clearing a table in the back when she began to feel lightheaded. She put the cleaning tray on the table and sat down. Shirley was taking an order to a booth when she saw Mabel sitting at the table. She gave the couple their order then walked over to Mabel and asked, "Are you all right?"

"I was feeling a little lightheaded," Mabel answered. "I'll be okay. I just need to sit here for a minute."

Jake rang the bell and yelled, "Order up."

Shirley was talking to Mabel and didn't hear the bell or Jake. "Did you take your blood pressure medicine this morning?" she asked.

"I took it, but my pressure's been running a little high the past couple of days."

"Then you need to go see your doctor." Shirley sat in a chair at the table.

"I have an appointment the day after Christmas."

Not hearing Mabel or Shirley, Jake walked out the kitchen and looked around the café. He spotted them at the table near the back. He knew something was wrong, so he checked the ticket on the two hamburger platters and took the platters to the two young men sitting at the counter. Then he hurried over to the back table. Bryant saw the concerned look on Jake's face when Jake walked by, so he turned around to see what was going on. He could see that Mabel wasn't feeling well, so he got up and walked to the back table. By the time Bryant got to the table, Jake was on his cell phone talking to her husband. "Willie's on his way," Jake said after hanging up the phone.

Bryant helped Mabel to a table near the front door, while Shirley gathered Mabel's coat and purse from the back office. Jake sat in the other chair at the table. "Thank you, Baby," Mabel told Bryant. "You know, if I was twenty years younger..."

"You'd still be too old for him," Jake cut her off. "Now sit down. I done told you, you're a retired cougar."

Mabel laughed. "If you didn't sound like Pearlie Mae then." She looked at Bryant. "Jake's wife Pearlie Mae was my best friend, and I been working in this café since the day she opened it. That's the only reason Jake ain't fired me."

"That's not the only reason," Jake countered. "I ain't fired you because you can run this place better than me."

"Then you need to start paying me better than what you do." Shirley walked up with Mabel's purse and coat. Bryant extended his arm as a crutch to help Mabel stand. Shirley helped her put on the coat and then handed her the purse. "Thank you, Sugah."

Bryant took his phone out of his pocket then asked Mabel if he could take a picture with her. She said she was happy too. "Are you gonna put me on that Facebook?" Mabel asked before she posed for the picture.

"Can I?"

"Of course, you can. Let everybody wonder who that fox you with."

"You should get in the picture too, Mr. Jake," Bryant suggested.

"I'll take the picture," Shirley said and reached for the phone.

Bryant and Jake leaned in close to Mabel and Shirley took the picture.

A few minutes later, Willie's car pulled up to the curb. Willie parked and turned on his hazard lights. With Jake and Bryant on both sides of her, Mabel met Willie at the door. "Watch this," Mabel whispered to Jake and Bryant.

"Mabel, are you all right?" Willie opened the door and asked.

"I will be," she responded then looked up at the mistletoe hanging above the door. "You see that, don't you?" She leaned toward him and waited for him to kiss her.

Willie looked at Jake and Shirley then asked, "She planned this, didn't she?"

"I don't think..." Shirley started to say when Jake over spoke her.

"You know she did," Jake revealed.

"I knew it," Willie said. "I ought to..."

Mabel grabbed him and pulled him to her. "Man, just kiss me," she ordered him. He obeyed and kissed her. "That's what I'm talking about." Willie took her by the hand and put his arm around her.

"Willie, call me if you need me," Jake said.

"I will," Willie responded.

After that, the day began to pass slowly again. Bryant skimmed through the *Chicago Defender* again and read articles he bypassed during the first reading. He checked his email and Facebook page again. Taylor had posted a live video of Samantha, Kyle, and Kyle Jr. arriving at their mother's house. Talia commented she was on her way. He was about to comment too but changed his mind.

Two hours later, as the afternoon turned into early evening, the world outside the café was shutting down for Christmas. Inside the café, a young lady sat at the counter drinking a cup of hot chocolate. She had been standing at the bus stop when she decided to come inside. And Bryant was still sitting in the booth by the window. He had just finished a hamburger and fries platter when Jake walked out the kitchen and over to the booth. "I just got off the phone with Mabel. She said her blood pressure's gone down and she's feeling a lot better."

"That's good to hear."

"Ever since you got here this morning, I've been trying to remember what Cassie said her husband's name was, so I asked Shirley. She said it's Malcolm."

Bryant remembered the name when he heard it. "She's right. It's Malcolm."

"Do you think Cassie's coming?" Jake asked.

"I know she's not. But I still can't make myself leave. Do you think that's crazy?"

"If it's crazy, I'm crazy," Jake answered. "I could've and probably should have retired by now, but I'm at this café five, six, sometimes seven days a week waiting for Pearlie Mae to walk out that kitchen, play a song on the jukebox, then put that little wag in her walk when the song comes on. Every time a customer walks through that door, I wait to hear her say, Welcome to Pearlie Mae's. And when I'm in the kitchen cooking, I don't have to wait. I can hear her standing there yelling at me for not fixing the scrambled eggs, the hash browns, the hamburgers, the toast, and everything else the way she showed me. My wife loved this place, and she put her all into it. She's been gone seven years, but I can still feel her when I'm here. Mabel was here with her from the start and having her here helps keep the café like it was when Pearlie Mae was here. Mabel should've given it up a few years back, but I think she stays on for me. I reckon I'm gonna have to fire her to make her sit on down."

After hearing this, Bryant felt better about being at the café.

The sun had set and the sidewalks and streets outside the café were nearly deserted. Taylor got out the car and walked up to the café. He could see Bryant, the café's only customer, sitting in a booth by the window. Bryant was reading something on his phone and didn't see Taylor walk up to the door.

Jake was sitting at the register, tallying up the day's receipts. "Welcome to Pearlie Mae's," Jake said when Taylor opened the door and walked in. Bryant looked up and saw Taylor.

"Hi," Taylor said. "I'm Bryant's brother, and I just stopped by to check on him."

"Pleased to meet you, Taylor. I'm Jake."

Bryant walked up to Taylor. "What's up?"

"I just stopped by to how you were doing," Taylor answered. "Okay. I'll tell the truth. Mom sent me."

Bryant shook his head disbelievingly. "I can't believe Mom sent you down here." Bryant grinned. "And you came!"

"What did you think I was going to do?" Taylor followed Bryant to the booth, and they sat down.

Shirley walked out the kitchen putting on her coat. "Uncle Jake, are you sure you don't want me to stay until you close?"

"No, you go ahead," he answered. "I'll be closing shop at eight – that's thirty more minutes. I done cleaned up the kitchen, so if anybody comes in, before eight, they're out of luck. And then Officer McKnight's parked across the street."

Shirley looked out the window and saw the police car parked on the curb. "All right then. I'll see you at Mom's house tomorrow." Shirley started out the door but stopped and turned to Bryant. "I'm sorry Cassie didn't show up," she said.

Bryant nodded then told her, "Have a merry Christmas."

"You too." She walked out the door.

Jake walked over to the jukebox. "You fellows don't mind if I play a song or two before I close up, do you?"

"No sir," Taylor answered.

Jake put the quarters in the jukebox and punched the code for five songs. The first song, "Baby Can I Change My Mind," by Tyrone Davis came on. Jake hummed and finger popped his way back to the counter.

Taylor looked at Bryant and joked, "I hope you've changed your mind." Bryant frowned and Taylor told him, "Man, I'm teasing."

Bryant turned and stared out the window.

"Are you all right?" Taylor asked.

Bryant slid the envelope over to Taylor, who opened it and took Cassie's wedding photo out. Taylor was about to say something when Bryant said, "Don't."

The five songs and the next thirty minutes passed quickly.

As the last song played, Betty Swan's "Make Me Yours," Jake began turning out the lights, Bryant and Taylor started toward the door. "I enjoyed your company today," Jake told Bryant.

"Thanks for putting up with me," Bryant said.

"You don't have to wait until next Christmas Eve to stop by," Jake said. "Whenever you're in town, drop in and see us."

"I will."

"It was good meeting you, Mr. Jake," Taylor said.

"Same here." Jake waved bye. "You fellows, have a merry Christmas."

Taylor's Mustang was parked in front of his mother's car. They got in the cars and drove away. Taylor first.

Chapter 20

The heart does not think. Thinking is what the mind does. Bryant knew this to be true. With that truth came the learning that the heart is only capable of loving, nothing else, and if not for the mind's manipulation, it would love without end. That was why none of his previous relationships worked and why he'd never fallen in love. His mind constantly wondered if there was someone better or more right for him. And then there were the questions. Will this work? What if it doesn't? Do I really love her? The constant worrying confused his heart, hindering and preventing it from loving without constraints. That was before he met Cassie.

As Bryant lay in bed staring at Cassie's wedding photo, he reminisced about meeting her last Christmas Eve. His mind had either taken a vacation that day or was asleep on the job. When he first saw Cassie get out her car and walk in the café, his mind should have thrown up a few roadblocks. But it didn't. There was no wondering, no questions, no warning not to follow her inside. A cease and desist order should have been issued, especially when she told him she had a fiancé. When he vowed to wait for her then kissed her under the mistletoe his mind should have done something instead of sitting idly by and letting him fall.

Now, after she didn't show up at the cafe, his mind was beginning to pose questions that set up checkpoints his heart passed a year ago.

~~~~~

Christmas Day passed as usual.

First thing that morning, Samantha, Kyle and Kyle Jr. arrived. Samantha knocked on Taylor and Bryant's bedroom door and woke them up. About an hour later, Talia arrived. Once everyone was there, they exchanged presents. Bryant's mother adored the Michael Kors handbag, but told him he had spent too much for it. "I'll feel funny walking around with a purse that cost this much," she said.

"I won't," Talia stated. Talia loved the bath and body soap, oils, and body spray set he had gotten her, but she was still willing to take the purse off her mother's hands. Samantha and Kyle loved their matching sweaters. Kyle Jr.'s favorite toy was the battery-powered car. And Taylor was ecstatic when he saw the two Play Station games Bryant bought him. Bryant loved his gifts too. His mother bought him two sweaters. Talia gave him a cologne set. Kyle and Samantha's presents were two loungewear sets and matching slippers.

And Taylor gave him screenwriting software with a note that read, "You've always wanted to write a screenplay. Start writing." He didn't have the heart to tell Taylor that he had bought the same screenwriting software a year earlier and it was still unopened on his desk.

After the presents were opened, Felicia and Samantha headed to the kitchen to finish dinner. The rest of them went outside to watch Kyle Jr. ride the car in the driveway. Talia used the remote control to guide the car, but she wasn't very good at it. She did a fine job of steering the car straight ahead, but when it came time to turn, she would either turn too wide and the car would end up off the driveway or she couldn't make it turn at all. When they laughed, she blamed the problems on the remote control. "Laugh all you want to, but I bet neither one you can do any better," she challenged them. Bryant did his best to enjoy the moment, but every few minutes Cassie would cross his mind. He wondered how her Christmas Day was going. Was she in Chicago or did they go home to Memphis? If they were in Chicago, did she at least drive by the café yesterday to see if he was there waiting for her like he said he would? Was she happy with her husband? He was asking himself these questions, when Talia handed him the remote and said, "Let's see how well you drive."

"Watch this," Bryant responded and took the remote. "I should be driving for NASCAR." Bryant guided the car down the driveway then turned and came back.

"Looks like the remote is working fine," Taylor pointed out.

"It wasn't when I had it," Talia snapped back.

Kyle Jr. laughed when Bryant made the car turn around in circles. His nephew's laughter was contagious and just what he needed to get her off of his mind. He began to have fun. But as soon as they went inside and started getting ready for dinner, she checked back in.

That night, after everyone had gone, Bryant and Taylor were in the den playing the new Play Station games when their mother walked in and sat down. "What time do we need to leave in the morning?" she asked Bryant.

"My flight's at 12:15, so let's leave at 9:00," he answered. "The day after Christmas is usually busy, so I need to be there a little early."

"Is this one of the new games you got Taylor?" she asked.

He answered, "Yes ma'am."

She sat quietly and watched them play the game. Bryant felt like she wanted to say something but wasn't sure how to. Right when it seemed she was ready to speak, Taylor blurted out, "Mom, since Bryant's got a new girlfriend, I'm going to get you a boyfriend for Christmas. And, I already know who."

"Sit down somewhere with that silliness," she brushed his statement off as nonsense.

"Yeah, you better watch your mouth talking to her like that," Bryant said, his tone unapologetically serious.

"What the...?" Taylor paused the game and sat up in the chair. "I didn't say anything disrespectful and I wouldn't. But what do you mean, I better watch my mouth?"

"He was just teasing," Felicia intervened.

"His tone wasn't teasing."

Felicia and Taylor both turned to Bryant and waited for him to respond.

"I'm sorry," Bryant said. He extended his fist to Taylor. "We're still cool, right?"

"Yeah, we're cool." Taylor dapped him up.

Felicia patted Bryant on the shoulder and said, "I've been meaning to apologize to you for sending Taylor to the café yesterday, but you had been gone all day and I was worried."

"I know why you sent him, and it's okay."

"Well, you never did tell me what happened."

Bryant began by telling her what she had already assumed – that Cassie didn't show up. He went on to tell her what Jake had told him about Cassie stopping by the café a few times after the day they met there. She said being at the café made her feel close to him. He told her about the wedding photo she sent with no return address and how she had not been back to the café since she got married. When he was done telling her what had transpired at the café, she asked, "So, what are you going to do now that she's married?"

Taylor, who had been quietly listening, wanted to know too. "Bryant?"

After a long, studied pause, Bryant responded, "I don't know what I'm going to do, but I have 364 days to think about it."

The Following Year

Chapter 21

Cassie's day started three hours before sunrise. She woke up and turned the alarm clock off before it rang. She showered and got dressed. Outside, the temperature was hovering in the low teens, so she put on a light sweater then her coat. She wrapped a scarf around neck, then she slipped on her gloves. It was 4:17 when she stepped out into the frigid January air, locked the front door behind her, got in her black Toyota Corolla, and started the twenty-minute drive to the hospital. She clocked in at 4:50 and began reviewing nursing plans for patients having out-patient surgery. Next, she prepared the pre-op rooms. As patients checked-in and were brought to the surgical prep room, she discussed the patient's procedure with them and answered any questions they had. Then she assessed the patients' vitals and prepped the patients for surgery.

Cassie's father was a hospital administrator and her mother a pharmacist, so she had grown up understanding the importance of providing proper healthcare to her patients. While she was working, she didn't allow herself to spend too much time thinking about anything other than caring for her patients and doing her job as best she could. If she caught herself worrying about what Malcolm might be doing while he was away, like she did while prepping the pre-op rooms, she quickly dismissed the thoughts. If thinking about a photo of Bryant with Jake and Mabel at Pearlie Mae's Café on Christmas Eve brought a smile to her face like it did before her last patient, Peter Gates, went into surgery, she enjoyed the bliss for a few seconds before she remembered where she was and what she was doing.

Peter, in his mid-fifties, was having a heart catherization. He had not spoken a word since he was brought to the pre-op room. Cassie took his blood pressure, inserted an intravenous line in his left arm, and gave him a pill to help him relax and still not one word. He remained silent even as a male nurse shaved his groin area. But, after seeing a smile sneak onto Cassie's face and watching her hurriedly wipe it away, he finally spoke. "I was feeling a little uneasy, but I feel a whole lot better now that I've seen you smile."

"Who, me?" she asked.

"Yes you," Peter responded.

Cassie grinned. "I'm sorry," Mr. Gates. "I was just thinking about..."

He cut her off, "Thank him for me."

"Who?"

"The fellow who put that smile on your face."

Later, after her patients were out of surgery, she monitored them through recovery. Before being discharged, she instructed them and their family on at-home, post-operative care. Twenty-six minutes after her last patient, Peter, was discharged from the Cath Lab, Cassie clocked out – exactly twelve hours and ten minutes after she clocked in.

Cassie wasn't in a hurry to get to the apartment because she would be there by herself. Malcolm had flown to Memphis two days ago to help manage the opening of a new warehouse and distribution center. The center was supposed to open back in October, but bad weather and construction issues delayed the opening four months. The company sent Malcolm down to ensure the opening went as planned. Malcolm was moving up in the company, and she was happy for him – for them, but she hated when he left her and went away for work.

As she drove past the road she should have turned on, she stretched – holding the steering wheel with her left hand and stretching her right arm then doing the same with her right hand and left arm. She expected Malcolm to call at any minute because he knew she was working twelve-hour shifts and was just getting off. She hoped today was one of the times he got busy and wasn't able to call until later. Because Malcolm was away, she had finally given in to the urge to just drive by Pearlie Mae's Café. She had not been to the café or even driven by since she married Malcolm because she didn't want to feel she was being unfaithful, even if it was only in her heart. She was determined to stay away from the café, and never considered driving by until Christmas Eve. She felt the urge to drive by the café slowly building throughout the month of December. Her anxiety peaked Christmas Eve. She didn't have to work, but she woke up around 3:30 and started getting dressed. Malcolm woke up and asked her where she was going, and she said she was going to work. He reminded her that it was Christmas Eve and she was off. It took her a minute to grasp what he was saying. When she did, she grinned and said she must have slept so hard, she woke up crazy. Malcolm asked her to come back to bed, but she said she couldn't go back to sleep and was going to watch television in the living room. She went in the living room, turned on the television, then went in the kitchen to make a cup of hot chocolate. Her anxiety worsened as the day progressed. She couldn't sit still or be in the same room with Malcolm. Her mother called around noon, and Cassie rambled to the point Margaret asked if she was all right. Cassie said she was fine, but Margaret didn't believe her and asked her to put Malcolm on the phone. When Malcolm got on the phone, Margaret asked him was everything okay. He told her yes, but Cassie had been acting a little out of the ordinary since she woke up getting dressed for work when she was off. Margaret told Malcolm to keep an eye on Cassie, and if he needed to, to call her back. After she hung up with her mother, she tried hard to fight her anxiety. Finally, she figured the best way to calm down was to drive by the café and see if Bryant was there. So, she concocted a reason to leave the house.

She walked in the living room putting her coat on. Malcolm was lying on the sofa watching a college football game. He looked up and asked, "Where are you going?"

"To the grocery store," she answered. "I'll be right back." She tried to make it to the door and leave before Malcolm decided to go with her. She didn't make it.

"Hold on," he said. "I'll go with you." He grabbed his coat and followed her out the door.

She didn't give up though. On their way to the store, she mentioned the accident she had last Christmas Eve and how she was thinking about driving by the intersection, but Malcolm didn't think it was a good idea.

"Why would you want to do that?" he asked.

"I was just feeling thankful that everyone was okay," she responded.

"You can be thankful without having to go back and relive it," he said.

They went to the store, shopped for a few things she didn't need, then went back to the apartment. She spent the rest of the day wishing she was at Pearlie Mae's or at least driving by, and Malcolm spent the rest of the day trying to figure out what was wrong with her. Later that night, after Malcolm went to bed, she did something she had not done since she got married. She turned on her laptop and went straight to Bryant's Facebook page. His posts were all public, so she could view them. Relief from the torment she had endured all day came when she saw the picture Bryant posted of him with Jake and Mabel at the café earlier that day.

A month later, the urge to drive past the café was back, but it wasn't as strong as it had been Christmas Eve. Cassie decided to act on it this time, because she knew Bryant wasn't at the café and because Malcolm wasn't in Chicago. As she pulled up to the intersection of Malloy and Porter's, she could see inside the café. The light was green, so she continued through the intersection then pulled to the curb across the street from the café. The café was busier than she had seen it before. Two couples were seated in her and Bryant's booth. She saw Shirley waiting on three customers at the counter, and two waitresses she didn't know serving customers at the booths and tables. As she watched the going-on inside the café, she thought about Bryant and the photo he'd posted of him, Mabel, and Jake. She wished she could have been there when the picture was taken. Cassie didn't feel she was cheating on Malcolm by parking across the street from the café where she met Bryant. If she hadn't been there reminiscing about meeting Bryant, she would've been home worrying about what Malcolm was doing in Memphis and who he was doing it with. She might have sat there until the café closed if a city bus had not pulled up behind her and flashed its headlights because she was blocking the bus stop. She put the car in drive and headed home to the apartment where no one was waiting for her.

Chapter 22

Bryant always had a career plan that influenced all his other life plans. He knew he wanted to be a journalist after joining his middle school's student newspaper. He was driven to succeed. After he graduated summa cum laude with a degree in journalism, he became a full-time reporter for the *Chicago Defender*. He put his all into the job and hardly had time for anything or anyone in his life except for his family. He was involved in a few relationships that didn't work, mostly because he didn't have time to make them work. But that wasn't the way he saw the breakups. He was convinced the relationships were doomed from the start because none of the women were the one – the woman who fit perfectly in his life. That's why his family was so surprised when he fell for Cassie, a woman he had not spent enough time with to know her last name. Cassie had become the only woman in his life. It didn't seem to matter that she was merely a memory replaying over and over in his head. When Bryant returned to Atlanta the day after Christmas, he put her wedding picture in a frame and placed it on his desk beside the framed selfie photo they took the day they met. Now that he knew she was married he was determined not to spend every waking day thinking about her and what could have been. Working was one of the few ways he could take a break from constantly thinking about her, so his New Year's resolution was to throw himself into his work and broaden his career and network.

When he first decided to move to Atlanta, he created a five-year career plan. He applied for and accepted the reporter position at the *Marietta Daily Journal* with the goal of working at the Metro Atlanta newspaper a couple of years and then moving to Atlanta's major daily, the *Atlanta Journal Constitution*. He gave himself five years. It took three. In March, he responded to a Journal Constitution job posting for a general assignment reporter. Two weeks later, he was interviewed by the newspaper's news editor and managing editor. Both were already familiar with his work for the Daily Journal. Two days later, the managing editor called and offered him the position.

The AJC's newsroom was busier than the Daily Journal's newsroom, which Bryant considered a good thing. It didn't give him as much time to think about things that weren't relevant to the job or the articles he was working on. The new position involved enterprise reporting, so if he wasn't working on assigned stories, he was talking to sources and conducting research to find stories that were newsworthy, about to break, or just needed to be told. He enjoyed working with his editor, Sheila Patterson, who reminded him of his sister Samantha. They both had take-charge personalities. Sheila was extremely supportive, which made for a smooth transition into his new position. She even helped him land his first freelance writing assignment for a national magazine.

The one drawback about the job at the AJC was the longer drive from his apartment in Marietta to the Journal-Constitution's office in Dunwoody, twenty miles away. While at the Daily Journal, his commute to the office was six miles without having to get on the interstate. Now, his commute was twenty miles of bumper-to-bumper traffic along two interstates. He thought he could cut down on the hour-long commute on the interstates by taking a couple of local highways. His first and only attempt at using local highways to cut down on his commute took nearly twice as long as the hour commute on the interstates. He also spent a lot more time traveling from one point to another because of the AJC's larger coverage area, which meant he spent even more time in the car, alone with thoughts of her and all the "what ifs" he could imagine.

He still managed to find time to hang out with John and Cal. Friday, they invited him to an Atlanta Hawks basketball game after work. He bet Cal the Hawks would beat the Celtics and lost twenty dollars. Following the game, they drove back to Cobb County and stopped by Caesar's Sports Bar for a nightcap. They were there about forty-five minutes when John's wife called and asked him to come home because the baby, a year old now, had a fever and might need to go the emergency room. John left in a hurry. By the time Bryant and Cal made it outside, John's car was nowhere to be seen. As soon as Bryant made it home, he sat at his desk and called John to see if John Jr. was okay. John told him the baby's temperature had gone down, so they didn't have to go to the emergency room. Before hanging up, he advised them to keep a close watch on John Jr. and to continue checking his temperature.

She was waiting for Bryant to hang up the phone. As he laid the phone on the desk, his eyes turned to her framed wedding photo and their framed selfie. He wondered what she was doing – if she and Malcolm had gone out because it was Friday night. But then again, he thought, she may have had a busy week and decided to stay in and catch up on her rest. If that was the case, he wanted to know whether she was lying in bed next to Malcolm or lying in bed alone because he was away for work. As much as Bryant loathed the thought of her with someone else, he prayed she was happy, and that joy filled her life, even if her life was with Malcolm and not him. He believed Cassie was pleased with the decisions she'd made and the life she was living. But not always.

He felt connected to her the day they met, and he believed he could sense when she was troubled and unhappy. As he was driving to State Farm Arena for the Hawks basketball game, he started to sense something was not right with her. The uneasiness brewed during the game, then intensified while he was at the bar. By the time he sat down at the desk and called John, he felt like an empath engulfed by feelings of deep sadness, rejection, anger, and regret. He knew these feelings were not his, that they belonged to the woman whose eyes appeared to beckon him from the two photos on his desk. He had no proof that she was feeling unhappy or that something was going terribly wrong in her life or that what he was feeling had anything to do with her. Still, there was no doubt in his mind he was feeling her heart break. Bryant showered and got ready for bed, but he still could not shake the nagging feeling that she was hurting, and he was helpless to do anything about it.

Chapter 23

Cassie clocked out on the computer at the nurse's station. She had completed another twelve-hour workday and was ready to go home and take a hot bath and quick nap before Malcolm made it back from Memphis. There was another reason she was glad to be off the clock. She had put it off her mind while she was working, but she was ready to pick up where she left off being angry at Malcolm and his constant trips to Memphis. She knew the trips were job-related, but it had gotten to the point where Malcolm was flying to Memphis for a few days every other week. While he was gone, she mostly worked and moped around the apartment. She knew a handful of people she worked with, but she hadn't become friendly enough with any of them to really hang out together. So, she gathered her umbrella and shoulder bag, told the other two nurses, Raynard and Leslie, she would see them Monday, then she started down the hallway. As she walked toward the staff exit, she took her cell phone out of her shoulder bag to check for any messages. There was a text message from Malcolm. She clicked on the message to open it.

I called you. Knew you wouldn't answer. Staying over another night. Explained in voice message, he texted.

Cassie stopped in her tracks. She read the message again.

I called you. Knew you wouldn't answer. Staying over another night. Explained in voice message.

Her finger's trembled as she checked her voice messages. There were two unheard messages. She listened to the first. It was a message from her mother. She pressed the key to save the message before it finished. The second message started.

"Hey Bae. The project we were working on ran into a snag, so we didn't get the system up and running. So, I'm sorry to have to tell you that I'll be here until tomorrow. I know you're disappointed, but I have to be here until the new system is operative. I'll call you later or you can call me when you get this message."

She pressed a key to replay the message.

"Hey Bae. The project we were working on ran into a snag, so we didn't get the system up and running. So, I'm sorry to have to tell you that I'll be here until tomorrow. I know you're disappointed, but I have to be here until the new system is operative. I'll call you later or you can call me when you get this message."

She pressed the key to save the message then dialed his number. His phone rang, and rang, and rang, but he didn't answer. She hung up before his voice recording came on. She dialed his number again, and his phone rang, and rang, and rang. She mashed the end-call key and dropped the cell phone in her bag. She opened her umbrella then pushed the door open and stepped outside, where the last waves of rain trailed the gray skies ahead of them.

As Cassie drove past the turn leading to her route home, the storm clouds started to clear, but the twilight was still darker than most nights. She was almost at her destination when her cell phone rang. She dug it out of her bag, which was on the passenger seat, and answered it with a cheerful, "Hello."

"Hey Bae," Malcolm said on the other end. "I was in a meeting when you called."

"I figured that," she responded.

"How was your day?" he asked.

"It was long, as usual, but surgery went well for all of my patients. How was your day?"

"We didn't get halfway done. There were some technical issues that were out of our control, so we won't be able to get the new system up and running until tomorrow. I left a message telling you that."

"I heard it. That's why I called you."

"Bae, I'm really sorry, but I'll make it up to you as soon as I get home tomorrow evening."

"I'll be waiting."

"You know, I hate leaving you home by yourself all the time, but I promise it won't be like this much longer."

"Don't worry about me. You just hurry up and get that system running so you can come home. I'm about to go inside, take a shower, and curl up on the sofa."

She veered into the lane leading to the airport.

"Well, I'll let you go inside and get settled," he said. "But I want you to call me and let me know what I'm missing."

"I will." She grinned. "Love you."

"Love you too."

An hour later, she stepped up to the ticket counter at the airport and purchased a ticket to Memphis.

Two hours later, she stepped off the plane at Memphis International Airport. After picking up the car she reserved while waiting for her flight in Chicago, she headed for the hotel Malcolm usually stayed in while working in Memphis. As she drove to the hotel, she thought about what she was going to say to Malcolm if she didn't catch him doing what she suspected he was doing. She had no idea what she would say if she did. One of the first things she wanted to ask him was why they both had to move to Chicago if he was going to be spending half his time in Memphis. If she had stayed in Memphis and he moved to Chicago, the amount of time they spent together would be about the same. And, when he left for Chicago, she would still be home with her family and friends.

Malcolm was driving a rental car too, so there was no use in scanning the hotel's parking lot for his car. Cassie knew the hotel would not give her Malcolm's room number, not without calling him first, which she didn't want. If someone was with him, he would simply have them leave another way. So, she parked the car, went inside, and purchased a room for the night. When the desk clerk asked about her luggage, she told him she had gotten separated from her husband on the highway and her luggage was in his car. It was a few minutes after midnight when she sat in a chair in the lobby and waited to catch him leaving with her or coming in after spending the night with her. After an hour or so, the desk clerk asked her if her husband was still coming, and she told him yes. Another hour passed. And then another. When the desk clerk approached her again, before he could speak, she reminded him that she had purchased a room in the hotel and was a guest waiting for her husband to get there. He went back to the counter and continued to keep a suspicious eye on her.

It was 5:38 that morning when the elevator doors opened and Malcolm stepped out the elevator holding hands with a woman, Anita – the same woman she had caught coming out of his apartment before they moved to Chicago. Cassie was staring right at him when Malcolm turned and saw her in the lobby. "Is the system up and running now, Malcolm?" The dam broke and tears flooded Cassie's eyes as she hurried toward the revolving doors.

"Cassie!" Malcolm ran into the revolving door behind her. "Cassie!"

Malcolm caught up with her as she raced toward the car. "Get away from me," she cried and snatched away from him. "I can't believe you! Why Malcolm? Why?"

"Cassie, I'm so sorry," he said and reached for her. She stepped back.

"You left me alone in Chicago to be here with another woman," she responded. "Do you think telling me you're sorry is going to make everything okay? I hate you for what you've done to me! To us!"

Malcolm cursed at himself as he watched Cassie get in the car and drive away.

Cassie could barely see the highway though her tears as she drove to her parents' house, which was about six miles from the hotel. But her tears could not blur the sight of Malcolm stepping out the elevator holding another woman's hand. She saw that clearly. Over and over, she watched the elevator doors open and Malcolm step out holding her hand. She was drawn to the look in his eyes before he saw her sitting in the lobby. His eyes conveyed the happiness he felt being with the woman. He was smiling, holding her hand, staring lovingly at her, even when he thought no one was looking. He didn't do that with her. At least not when it didn't serve a purpose.

She pulled in her parents' driveway and parked. Cassie hated having to tell her parents why she was in Memphis and what had just happened, but she needed someone to hold her and keep her from falling apart. She dialed her mother's number. She couldn't respond for crying when her mother answered the phone, "Hello."

"Who's that this time of morning?" Nathaniel rolled over and asked.

"Cassie, what's wrong?" Margaret yelled into the phone. "Cassie!"

Nathaniel snatched the phone from his wife. "Cassie! What's wrong?"

"In the driveway," she managed to say.

"The driveway?" Nathaniel asked.

Margaret sprang from the bed and over to the window. She looked outside and saw the car with the headlights still on in the driveway. "She's outside," Margaret yelled.

Nathaniel and Margaret raced down the stairs, opened the front door, and saw their daughter struggling to reach them before she drowned in her tears.

"Cassie!" Margaret burst into tears and threw her arms around her daughter.

"What happened, Baby?" her father asked.

"I caught him with her," she cried. "I caught him!"

Nathaniel watched Cassie's world crumble around her knowing there was nothing he could do to stop it. He choked back the tears as he put his arms around his daughter and wife and tried to shield them from any other mayhem that might be headed their way.

Chapter 24

To let her husband, Nathaniel, tell it, Chicago was like fire and ice. In the wintertime, he said, it got so cold that the words coming out of your mouth would freeze and fall to the ground before you finished saying them. And the summers were so hot, he said, the air scorched your nostrils when you breathed. Nathaniel had only been to Chicago once, and it was to help move Cassie and Malcolm there two years ago. That's when he told his wife why he never liked Chicago and why he wasn't too thrilled about their daughter moving there. Margaret brought this up when he found out Cassie and Darryl were flying to Chicago to bring her car, clothes, and other belongings back to Memphis, and he started packing a suitcase to go with them. She reminded him that it was July, and the city was experiencing a two-week heatwave that weather forecasters predicted would linger another week. That didn't stop him from packing. She asked and then pleaded with him to stay home with her, but he said nothing could stop him from being on that plane with his daughter and son the next day. Margaret finally gave up and told him they were catching the 12:24 American Airlines flight. He went online and purchased a seat on that same flight. Even though she did it for his own good – to keep him from getting in trouble when he finally saw Malcolm, that night Margaret prayed and asked God to forgive her for lying to her husband. Nathaniel pitched a hissy fit the next morning when he woke up and discovered Margaret had lied and Cassie and Darryl left on the 6:10 American Airlines flight while he was asleep.

Cassie had been in Memphis since the morning she caught Malcolm cheating. She could not tolerate seeing him or being in the apartment that was supposed to be their home, so she stayed at her parents' house and purchased whatever she needed. Malcolm called her so many times the day she caught him that she turned off her cell phone. He knew better than to go to her parents' house, because when he called their house phone, Nathaniel answered and promised to bury him alive when and wherever he saw him. A week later, he tried to apologize in a letter, but Cassie gave the unopened envelope back to the mailman and had it marked, "Return to Sender." Five weeks passed before she called Malcolm to let him know she was coming to get her things.

Malcolm was at the apartment when Darryl parked the U-Haul on the other side of Cassie's car. Cassie got out the U-Haul and was waiting for Darryl to get out. When he opened the door and got out the U-Haul grinning, she asked, "What's so funny?"

"Read this," he responded and handed her his cell phone. Cassie read their dad's text to Darryl.

If he looks at her wrong, knock his ass out! For me. Please, Nathaniel had written.

"You know he's fire hot at us for leaving him," Darryl confirmed what she already knew.

Cassie handed Darryl the phone. "He was already fire hot, and that's why we left him."

The front door of the apartment opened, and Malcolm stepped outside. Cassie stopped in her tracks. She had not seen him since that night at the hotel, but she could tell just by looking that the man standing in the doorway wasn't the man stepping out of a hotel elevator with another woman five weeks ago. The man she was staring at reminded her of the man she met during their sophomore year at the University of Memphis and began dating two months later. He appeared regretful and saddened because he had hurt and disappointed her. That was more like the loving and thoughtful Malcolm she met and nothing like the crass, self-regarding whoremonger she married.

"Cassie," he said as though he needed permission to speak to her. "It's good to see you." He waited for her to speak but she didn't say a word. "I know that you don't want to see or talk to me, so I'll stay out of your way."

She walked by him and went into the apartment.

"Darryl, let me know if you need me to help you move anything," Malcolm said.

"I will," Darryl said and followed Cassie inside.

Cassie packed her clothes into four suitcases and three garment bags, while Malcolm helped Darryl load the bedroom set and the television from the guest room in the U-Haul. Darryl and Malcolm loaded Cassie's computer, printer, desk, and exercise bike in the U-Haul next. As Cassie went around the apartment packing personal items, like books, framed photos, and CDs, it was hard to believe their seven-year relationship - five years of dating, a yearlong engagement, and a marriage that lasted a year and eleven days, had come to an end.

She was fed up when she decided to walk out the hospital, get on a plane to Memphis, and wait in a hotel lobby for proof that he was being unfaithful. Knowing there was more – a man out there who could love her and did love her the way Bryant did, had a lot to do with her getting on that plane. She had hardly thought about Bryant since that night because she was too busy hating Malcolm. As she got in her car, which Malcolm had brought to the apartment from the airport parking lot, she glanced in the rearview mirror at Malcolm standing on the sidewalk waving goodbye to Darryl in the U-Haul but staring piteously at her in the car. She couldn't believe he was really hurting, but she could not make herself care even if she wanted to.

Cassie and Darryl spent the night at a hotel. The next morning, she woke up wondering if she would ever see Bryant again now that she was about to leave Chicago. She felt he would show up at the café on Christmas Eve to wait for her just like he said he would, but she was moving to Memphis and wouldn't be here. Bryant was still on her mind when she got in her car and Darryl got in the U-Haul, and they pulled out the hotel's parking lot. After driving slowly by Pearlie Mae's Café twice with Darryl following her, Cassie turned on the highway leading to the interstate that would take them back to Memphis.

Chapter 25

Before Bryant left home for work on the rain-soaked first Monday in December, Sheila called and asked if he could pick up an assignment first thing that morning. The reporter who was supposed to cover the ribbon-cutting ceremony for the new Marta rail expansion into Henry County, south of Atlanta, called in from the hospital's emergency room. That meant Bryant would have to drive from Marietta, about twenty miles north of Atlanta, into and through the city, to the new station, about twenty-four miles south of the city. Because of the morning rush-hour traffic, Bryant gave himself two hours to get from his apartment to the station. He had made it through the city and was headed south when he started to see airplanes taking off from the airport. He thought about his next flight, which was nineteen days away or two days before Christmas.

He was not in the holiday spirit when he put up a Christmas tree in his apartment the day after Thanksgiving. Not possessing any holiday cheer was also the reason he had not gone Christmas shopping. This would not have been unusual for the before-Cassie Bryant, who waited until a few days before Christmas to buy gift cards for everyone. Cassie changed him and how he felt about the holidays. Last Christmas was the first time he put up a Christmas tree, and he went Christmas shopping for actual presents instead of the usual gift cards. Nearing the end of his year-long wait to get back to Pearlie Mae's Café on Christmas Eve, where Cassie might be, should've been enough to lift his spirits, but it wasn't. Knowing this was motivation enough to go through the motions of putting up a tree and planning to go shopping, but something was nagging at him, smothering his holiday spirit before it could catch fire. Bryant knew what it was. For the first time ever, he wasn't looking forward to going home for Christmas. If it had not been for his promise to Cassie – to wait for her at Pearlie Mae's Café on Christmas Eve, he probably would have made up an excuse, like having to work, to keep from going home, because he was having trouble accepting what he considered was the end of his parents' marriage. Back in September, he was covering a political campaign rally on Smyrna's Village Green when Taylor called. His phone was on silent mode, so he let it ring thinking Taylor would leave a message. As soon as the phone stopped ringing, Taylor called again. Bryant, figuring it was something important, walked away from the crowd then answered the phone, "What's up?"

Taylor responded, "I hate to ruin your day. Knowing you, maybe your life. But I have to tell you this."

"What's wrong?"

"You know Mom's got a Facebook page now."

"Yes. I got a friend request from her yesterday."

"Well, before you hear it from someone else or before Mom posts about it on Facebook." Taylor inhaled deeply then exhaled. "Are you ready for this?"

"Just tell me what you're talking about!"

"Mom's dating."

"Mom's what?"

"She's dating."

"Says who?"

"Says Mom," Taylor answered.

"How can Mom be dating?" Bryant asked. "And, dating who?"

"Deacon Hampton. They've been going out to dinner, movies, and church functions since me and Talia graduated."

"That was over a year ago, and you're just telling me?"

"Mom asked us not to tell you because you'd act just like you're acting now."

"How am I supposed to act? Mom's married!"

"Correction," Taylor said. "Mom is widowed and there's nothing wrong with her dating eleven years after her husband died."

Bryant hung up the phone. A few seconds later, his cell phone beeped. It was a text from Taylor. He opened the text message.

Remember how you acted when I joked about getting Mom a boyfriend for Christmas? You almost got punched then. That's why I didn't tell you.

Bryant thought about last Christmas when they were in the den and Taylor joked that he was going to get their mother a boyfriend for Christmas. He got upset with Taylor then, but he was even more upset now that he knew Taylor had been testing him to see how he felt about their mother dating. Bryant pressed the delete key.

Bryant usually called his mother once a week, sometimes twice, but after finding out she was dating a deacon from their church, he stopped calling. This didn't go unnoticed by his mother. She started calling him since he wouldn't call her. At first, he ignored her calls, forcing her to leave messages that he didn't acknowledge. This went on for three weeks. That's when Taylor called and threatened to come to Atlanta and make him call her back. As soon as Taylor hung up, Samantha called. She told him she was putting him on three-way so he could talk to their mother and she dared him to hang up. When their mother answered the phone, Samantha said, "Hi Mom. I have Bryant on the phone."

Bryant said hello to his mother and told her he had planned to call her when he got home that evening. She acted as though she believed him. She asked how he was doing and was he still coming home for Christmas. He said he was doing fine, and he would be home for Christmas. The conversation continued in this ask-and-answer manner until Bryant told them he had to hang up because the meeting he was covering was back in session.

In nineteen days he was going to be home for Christmas, and he didn't know what to expect with his family, who all supported his mother's dating, and with Cassie, because he had not felt connected to her in months – since the night he went to the Hawks basketball game with John and Cal back in May.

It was still raining when the ribbon-cutting ceremony ended, and Bryant got in the car and headed to the office. As soon as he was back on the interstate, he turned on the radio and heard his first holiday song of the year, Wham's "Last Christmas." He sang along, but he still wasn't feeling the Christmas spirit. He was planning to go Christmas shopping that weekend, and he hoped browsing through stores with his shopping list would do the trick.

Bryant woke up early Saturday morning so he could start his Christmas shopping. He ate breakfast, warmed-up pizza, at his desk in the living room. He grinned when he noticed the unopened screenwriting software Taylor had given him for Christmas was on the CD shelf next to the same unopened screenwriting software that he bought two years ago. He glanced down at Cassie's framed wedding photo and their framed selfie photo, which sat on the desk, and then at his first-ever Christmas shopping list that he made the night before. Everyone was on the list, which included two or three possible gift ideas for each person except Cassie. Her name was at the bottom of the list and the only gift listed for her was a bottle of Good Girl perfume. Last Christmas his mother asked him what he was going to do now that he knew Cassie was married. He told her he didn't know, but he had 364 days to decide.

That was what he said, not what he felt. When his mother asked, he already knew where he was going to be the following Christmas Eve – at Pearlie Mae's Café waiting for her. He didn't get Cassie a present last Christmas because he didn't really expect her to show up. Hearing about her visits to the café after the day they met and the pink envelope with her wedding photo strengthened his resolve. So, this year, he was more hopeful. But he still didn't foolishly think she would just walk through the café's door and say she was ready to live happily ever after with him.

The rain was followed by cooler weather, which made it feel more like December and the holiday season. Being from Chicago, he needed cold weather and snow to make it feel like Christmas. Although Cassie and the Good Girl perfume were at the bottom of the list, Macy's was his first stop because he knew he would find it there. As he waited at the perfume counter for the salesclerk, he heard a female voice call his name. He turned around and saw Rhena walking up to him.

"I see you're shopping for my Christmas present," she said. "What are you getting me?"

"You're going to have to wait until Christmas to see," he replied.

"Well, don't look silly when I show up at your apartment Christmas Day to pick up my gift."

"You better come a few days early since I'm going to Chicago for Christmas."

An awkward pause followed. They were not on the best of terms when he last saw her at a Marietta City Council workshop meeting about seven months earlier. Rhena was on the agenda to present a report on the city's community relations projects. She had not spoken to him in months after he told her he had met and fell in love with a girl named Cassie, whose last name he didn't know and who he'd only spent a couple of hours with one Christmas Eve. During the meeting, he took advantage of her professionalism and forced her to speak to him by posing questions about her report for the article he was writing. Afterwards, she caught up with him in the parking deck and told him, since he forced her to speak to him, she better have a direct quote or two in his article about the council workshop. He promised there would be and there was.

Rhena sprayed a fragrance tester in the air. "Nice." She placed the tester back on the counter then turned to Bryant. "So, you've moved on up from the Daily Journal to the Journal Constitution," she said.

"I have," he responded.

"And…?"

"It's busier because of the larger coverage area," he answered. "But I'm enjoying it."

The salesclerk walked back up to the counter with a bottle of Good Girl perfume. "Here you are," she said and handed him the box.

"Who's the lucky girl?" Rhena asked. "Or, is it still the woman you told me about?"

"It's still her."

Bryant could tell Rhena wanted to ask more questions like, had he seen her since the day they met. But instead of asking what she really wanted to know, she told Bryant, "I need to be going. It was good seeing you."

"You too," he said and watched her walk away.

Bryant looked at his shopping list and mentally checked Cassie's name off the list.

Chapter 26

There were two additional place settings on his mother's dining room table. Bryant pretended not to notice this as he walked through the dining room into the kitchen where his mother was taking grocery out of shopping bags and putting items in the refrigerator, cabinet, and pantry. His flight from Atlanta arrived at 6:35 the evening before Christmas Eve. Taylor was off from work, so he picked Bryant up at the airport. Snow had fallen continuously the past two days, and the city was a picturesque winter wonderland. The sun set before his flight landed, so the colorful lights and brightly shining ornaments dazzled against the pristine snow and the night sky. This was how Christmas was supposed to look, but it wasn't enough to put him in the Christmas spirit.

On the way from the airport, Bryant and Taylor tried to avoid talking about their mother because they were on opposing sides when it came to her dating Deacon Hampton. Bryant, who had been closer to their father, Sam, than Taylor and his two sisters, still saw their mother as their father's wife eleven years after his father's death. Taylor loved and missed their dad too, but he felt that after eleven years it was okay for their mother to date. So, they talked about other things, like how things were going on their jobs, Taylor deciding to call it quits with Jennifer, Talia's new boyfriend – an English professor at the university, and finally Cassie.

"Are you going to the café tomorrow?" Taylor asked after taking the exit ramp off the interstate.

"Yes," Bryant answered.

"Do you really think she's going to show up?"

"I don't know, but I'll be there if she does."

Taylor was having a hard time understanding Bryant's fascination – that's what he called it – with this woman he hardly knew. He glanced over at Bryant. "May I ask you something?"

"That's what you've been doing since I got in this car."

"Are you seeing anyone back in Atlanta?"

"I was," Bryant answered.

Taylor wanted to know more, so he probed deeper. "What happened? Why did you stop seeing her?"

"I told her about Cassie, and she broke up with me."

"You told her you've got this crazy thing for a woman you fell in love with at first sight and haven't seen since. What did you think was going to happen?"

"It wasn't love at first sight."

"Then love after ten minutes. Same thing!"

Bryant was a little annoyed, so he asked, "Can we find something else to talk about?"

Taylor obliged by not saying anything else the rest of the way to the house.

Their mother was at the grocery store when Taylor and Bryant pulled in the driveway. Bryant took his luggage upstairs to the guest room. A week ago, he shipped a box containing his presents for everyone to his mother's house. The box was on the bed. He unpacked the box then went back downstairs and placed the gift-wrapped presents under the Christmas tree. By then, Felicia had made it home and was in the kitchen.

"Mom," he called as he walked through the dining room on his way to the kitchen. The dining room table had already been set for Christmas dinner, and he tried not to notice the extra place settings on the table.

"Hi baby." She stopped putting groceries away and hugged Bryant. "I'm glad you're home."

"Me too." He started helping her put away the groceries. "Did you carry all these bags in yourself?"

"No," she answered. "Your brother helped me. Have you eaten anything?"

"No ma'am," he answered.

"I bought onion rolls and provolone cheese to make hot corned beef and pastrami hoagies. I even bought pickles and sour cream potato chips."

"You know that's my favorite meal in the whole world," he gushed "I got hungry just hearing you say corned beef and pastrami hoagies."

"Well, give me a few minutes," she said. "By the way. I know you're going to the café tomorrow, but I hope you make it back in time to go with us to the church's Christmas Eve program."

"We haven't been to the Christmas Eve program in years," Bryant thought out loud.

"I know," his mother acknowledged. "I hope you'll be able to make it."

Bryant was glad his mother wanted to attend the Christmas Eve program. Before her husband's death, she was active in their church. She was on several committees and head of the usher board. She even made sure her husband and children were actively involved in the church. That changed after her husband died. She still attended church regularly. She came, she listened, paid her tithes, took communion on the first Sunday, then went home. But she gave up her seat on the committees and boards. When asked about her renewed interest and participation in activities at church, she said it had a lot to do with all the free time she had since she retired.

"I'll try to be there." Bryant turned to walk out the kitchen and saw Taylor standing in the doorway.

Taylor smiled, pleased with what he overheard, and said, "Merry Christmas, big brother."

"Merry Christmas," Bryant replied and dapped Taylor on his way out the kitchen.

Chapter 27

It was Christmas Eve, and as soon as Bryant's feet hit the floor, he started getting dressed to go to the café. Twenty minutes later, he hurried down the stairs. There was a note on the hallway table where his mother kept her car keys. She had written the note to tell him she went with Deacon Hampton to IHOP for breakfast and that he could use her car. Taylor was still in bed when Bryant left for the café.

Jake, who was sitting on a stool at the register, smiled when he saw Bryant walking up the sidewalk toward the café. He stood and waited for Bryant to open the door. "You made it," Jake said as soon as Bryant entered.

"What happened to my 'Welcome to Pearlie Mae's'?" Bryant stopped at the door and asked.

Jake laughed. "Welcome to Pearlie Mae's!"

Bryant looked above the door. The mistletoe was there. Bryant smiled and walked up to the counter. "It's good to see you, Mr. Jake."

"Well, it's extra good to see you because me and Mabel made a little bet about whether or not you were going to show up. I bet you would."

"That means you won." Bryant looked around the café. "Where is Mrs. Mabel?"

"She was forced to retire," Jake answered.

"Because of her health?"

"No, her big mouth." Jake grinned. "I'm kidding. She gave it up back in February. It was time though. But don't worry. You'll get to see her. We betted and ain't no way she gonna pay up unless she sees you here with her own eyes."

A tall, bald man, who looked to be in his late-thirties or early-forties, walked out the kitchen. "Mr. Jake, Shirley told me to ask you if you wanted me to fix you anything?"

"No, I'm okay," Jake answered. He turned to Bryant. "I want you to meet one of our cooks, Eddie. And Eddie, I want you to meet my friend Bryant."

Eddie walked up to the counter, shook Bryant's hand, and asked, "How's it going?"

"I'm good," Bryant responded. "Looks like I'm about to be your first customer this morning."

"Are you ready to order?" Jake asked.

"Yes. I'll have a ham and cheese omelet, toast, a glass of apple juice, and a cup of coffee after my meal."

Jake wrote the order on a ticket and handed it to Eddie. As Eddie walked toward the kitchen, Bryant said, "It was nice meeting you, Eddie."

"Same here."

Bryant told Jake he was going to have a seat then walked over to the booth by the window, took off his coat, and sat down. He gazed out the window at the intersection. He remembered standing on the corner watching her get out her car then walk in the café and sit down in a window booth. He followed her in the café and sat across from her in the booth. She said her name was Cassie. That was Christmas Eve two years ago. Now, he was sitting in that same booth, staring out at the intersection, hoping she would walk through the door.

"Hello Bryant," Shirley said as she placed a glass of water and a glass of apple juice on the table.

Bryant, slightly startled, turned from the window. "Shirley."

"I didn't mean to scare you." She placed silverware on a napkin in front of him. "I might as well go ahead and tell you because you're going to find out as soon as Mrs. Mabel gets here."

"I heard about the bet," he replied. "Mr. Jake told me he won."

"He did."

Eddie rang the bell and yelled, "Order up!"

"I'll be right back." She returned with his breakfast. "Let me know when you're ready for your coffee."

A few more customers came in. Three sat at the counter, and four sat together two booths behind Bryant. Jake helped Shirley out by taking orders for the two policemen at the counter. Bryant watched as Jake worked behind the counter. He moved noticeably slower. His voice didn't carry like it had the last time Bryant was there. The years were finally catching up with him. After the three customers at the counter ate, paid their bill, and left, Bryant walked over to the counter and sat on a stool across from the register. He asked Jake how he was doing, and Jake told him it had been a rough year.

"I didn't have any major health issues, other than Father Time catching up to me," Jake elaborated. "I can't get around like I used to, but I try to help out as much as I can. My niece, Shirley, practically runs the place now. I just show up to hang out with my girl, Pearlie Mae."

"I'm glad you're still showing up."

"So, how's life been treating you, young man?" Jake asked.

"Pretty good," Bryant answered. "Back in the spring, I landed a job at the Journal Constitution, which is Atlanta's major daily."

"Congratulations."

"Thank you." Bryant was ready to ask Jake about Cassie the moment he walked in the café, but he decided to wait. He couldn't wait any longer. "Have you seen or heard from Cassie?"

"No, I haven't. Not since she sent the wedding picture."

Bryant was disappointed. Even if she didn't show up while he was there, he at least hoped she had stopped by the café or contacted Jake again. That would prove she was still thinking about him. Now, he wondered if she was happily married and had given up on the possibility of one day being with him.

"Don't look so down," Jake tried to encourage him. "That doesn't mean she's not going to show up."

The rest of the day passed slowly. Bryant went back to the booth and read the newspaper he bought from the vending rack. Then he used his cell phone to check his email and Facebook. Around 2:00, he ordered a grill cheese sandwich and a bowl of tomato soup. After he was done eating, he checked his email and Facebook again. He played a few songs on the jukebox then went and sat at the counter. As he listened to Jake reflect on the days when his wife ran the café, he kept glancing at the clock on the wall behind the counter.

"I see you're watching the clock," Jake said. "You got somewhere else you need to be?"

"My mom wants me to go with her to our church's Christmas Eve program at six," Bryant answered. "I really don't want to go, but I don't want to disappoint her."

"Why don't you want to go? So, you can sit here and wait for Cassie?"

"Yes, but that's part of the reason."

"What's the other part?"

"My mom has been seeing this deacon at the church, and..." Bryant hesitated.

"And you think your mom's too old for that kind of nonsense, right?"

"I don't think she's too old. She has a husband, my dad."

"Well, that makes a difference. Where is your dad?"

"He passed away," Bryant answered.

"When?"

"Eleven years ago."

"That makes a difference too." Jake enlightened him. "Listen son. I was married to my wife forty-one years. She's been gone seven. If I was ten or twenty years younger, Pearlie Mae wouldn't have wanted me to spend the rest of my life alone. She doesn't want that for me now, but she knows I'm seventy-four and can't do nobody any good. How old is your mom?"

"Fifty-eight."

"Oh man, she's way too young to spend the rest of her life by herself."

Bryant turned and gazed out the window. He knew Jake was right, but he still wasn't ready to accept his mother dating a man who was not his father.

Jake tapped on the counter to get Bryant's attention then asked, "I got a question for you?"

"What's that?"

"How does your mom feel about Cassie and about you being here?"

"She's worried, and thinks I'm setting myself up to be let down."

"This morning when you were leaving to come here, did she tell you not to come? Did she say you were wasting your time?"

"No. She wasn't home, but she left a note telling me to take her car."

"Ain't that something? Even though she's worried about you, she told you to take her car and drive to the café and wait for this married woman you hardly know."

"I hadn't thought about it like that," Bryant admitted.

"What you shared with Cassie was something that don't happen to too many people or too often. Now, it's a memory. A good one, and I don't blame you for trying to hold on to it. What your mom has with this deacon is real, whether it works out or not. It's real because he's here with her. It's been a while for your mom, so she's probably having a hard time adjusting to being in a relationship. I bet you she could use your support."

"You're right." Bryant looked at the clock. It was 4:20. "I need to go if I'm going to make it to the Christmas program on time."

Bryant paid his tab then stood at the counter and put on his coat.

"You're leaving?" Shirley asked, walking out the kitchen.

"My mom wants me to go to our church's Christmas Eve program with her."

Shirley pulled out her cell phone. "Mrs. Mabel hasn't made it here yet, so you better let me take a picture for proof."

"Please do that," Jake said. "Come on Bryant, so we can all three be in the picture."

"Do you want me to take it?" Eddie walked out the kitchen and asked.

Shirley handed him the phone and said, "Thanks."

Bryant handed him his phone too. "Take one with my phone too," he told Eddie.

Shirley posed between Bryant and Jake, and Eddie took three pictures on Shirley's phone and two on Bryant's phone. He handed them their phones, and they both looked at the pictures. "These are nice," they remarked at the same time.

"Well, I better be going," Bryant said and started toward the door.

"What if Cassie shows up?" Shirley asked.

Bryant reached inside his coat pocket and took out the gift-wrapped perfume. "Give her this," he said and handed Jake the present.

Jake put the present on a shelf behind the counter. "Now you hurry on home so you can help your mom have a Merry Christmas," he told Bryant.

Bryant walked out the café and over to his mother's car. He cranked the car and waited for the windshield to defrost. He hated leaving before the café closed, but Jake was right. He needed to be there for his mother. He was the only obstacle standing between her and happiness. He was ready to move. He put the car in drive and drove away.

~~~~~

Cassie saw him.

From the driver's seat of the black Mazda parked on the curb across the street, she saw him sitting at the counter talking to Jake. She saw him pay his tab, put on his coat, wave bye, and then get in the Infinity and drive away. She had sat in the car for nearly an hour debating whether to get out and go inside the café. She still hadn't decided when Bryant walked out the café, got in the car, and drove away. Now that he was gone and she didn't have to wonder what she was going to say to him, her mind and heart stopped racing. She thought about driving off, but she was compelled to go inside.

Jake saw her crossing the street. "Shirley," he called. "Shirley, come here." Shirley walked out the kitchen and immediately saw Cassie walking toward the café.

"Well, I'll be," Shirley said, shaking her head in disbelief. "And he just left."

"She saw him before he left," Jake said. "She got out that car parked across the street. It's been there for about an hour."

Cassie opened the door and walked in the café.

Jake and Shirley greeted her, "Welcome to Pearlie Mae's."

"Hi Mr. Jake. Shirley." She walked up to the counter. She looked the same, except her eyes were sadder than they used to be.

"Wow!" Shirley walked from behind the counter and hugged Cassie. "I can't believe you're here. You know Bryant just left."

"I saw him," Cassie confessed.

"Why didn't you let him know you were here?" Shirley asked.

"Because I'm not ready," she answered.

"It's good to see you, Cassie," Jake said. "How have you been?"

Cassie sat on a stool at the counter. "It's been a difficult year, but I'm still here."

Jake and Shirley noticed she was not wearing a wedding ring. When she saw them looking at her hand, she answered their question before they could ask it. "I divorced Malcolm," she divulged. "He was having an affair with an ex-girlfriend back home, and he was seeing her every time he flew to Memphis for work."

"Men can be so awful," Shirley said.

"Yes, they can," Cassie agreed. "Well, some men."

"Are you still here in Chicago?" Jake asked.

"No, sir. I moved back to Memphis in May. I flew in today." Cassie glanced over at the booth that she and Bryant had sat in. Tears formed in her eyes as she revealed, "I have to put me and my life back together before I talk to Bryant, but I really needed to see him sitting here waiting for me like he said he would."

"And he would still be here if his mother didn't need him," Jake said and handed her a napkin.

"Is everything all right?" Cassie asked as she wiped the tears from her eyes.

"He's just driving her to church," Jake answered then reached down on the shelf behind the counter and picked up the present Bryant had left. "He told me to give you this if I saw you." Jake placed the present on the counter in front of Cassie. "Merry Christmas."

Chapter 28

Trust issues.

Bryant woke up the next morning around 7:30 thinking how he had been wrong about trust issues. He pondered this as he lay in bed staring at the snow falling outside his bedroom window. No one was stirring in the house, so it was quiet enough for him to hear his thoughts. He relished quiet, still moments like this, when he could listen to what his heart and mind were feeling and saying. He thought about how he had waited for her at the café the past two Christmas Eves like he said he would, but she didn't show up. And, she had not been back to the café since she married. In Bryant's mind, this meant she was happily married and moving on with her life, which isn't what he expected because she had trust issues. He remembered that day in the café when she told him how she caused the accident at the intersection. She said she was driving and talking to Malcolm on the phone when he told her his flight had been cancelled and he wouldn't be able to make it back to Chicago that day. Upset and distracted, she ran the stoplight and hit two other vehicles. What caused Bryant's eyebrows to raise was her assumption that something other than the weather was preventing Malcolm from flying back to Chicago to be with her. When he told her about the weather forecast for the Georgia and Tennessee region, she seemed relieved that she could believe what Malcolm said. Bryant saw this as a tell-tale sign there were trust issues in their relationship, and he expected their marriage to fall victim to those issues. This gave Bryant hope and drew him back to the café every year, every Christmas. But now, the Christmas Eve he spent with Cassie was beginning to feel distant and imagined like a dream. And this morning, as he lay in bed staring out the window and listening to his thoughts, he began to realize the futility of trying to recapture a dream once you wake up.

Bryant heard his mother walk past his bedroom door and down the stairs. She was humming a song he heard the choir sing at the church's Christmas Eve program. He could hear the happiness in her voice. Bryant smiled. He was glad he listened to Jake and went to the program. When he made it home from the café, they didn't have to ask if Cassie showed up. His solemn expression told them she didn't. He took a shower and got dressed, then he drove his mother to church. Taylor rode with them. Talia and her new boyfriend, Lawrence, were sitting next to Samantha, Kyle, and Kyle Jr. when Bryant, Taylor, and Felicia walked in the church. Bryant took his mother by the hand and walked her down to the empty seats beside Talia. Deacon Hampton, who was sitting in the deacons' section, waved at Felicia. Bryant grinned when he saw his mother's girlish smile when she waved back. As he sat through the program, he could not help but wonder what was going on at the café. He felt, because he had left the café early and not stayed until closing, that he had not fulfilled his vow to be there waiting for her.

While they were having refreshments in the fellowship hall, Deacon Hampton came over to the table and sat beside Felicia. Bryant and his family met Deacon Hampton more than twenty years ago when they first joined the church. Bryant's dad and Mr. Hampton, what they called him at the time, became church deacons a year before Bryant's dad died. Bryant had not seen Deacon Hampton since the Sunday after Taylor and Talia's college graduation when the family attended church together.

They talked briefly, mostly about what Bryant was doing in Atlanta. That was a year and a half ago. Their conversation after the Christmas program was pretty much the same, except now he had to remember he wasn't just talking to a deacon at his family's church, he was talking to the man dating his mother.

Bryant was still lying in bed when his mother called for him and Taylor to come downstairs. She wanted them to shovel snow off the walkway and the driveway so Samantha and the others wouldn't have a problem parking. Bryant and Taylor went back upstairs and got dressed to go outside and clear the driveway. Only a few inches of snow had fallen, so it didn't take long for Bryant and Taylor to clear the snow and sprinkle salt on the driveway and walkway.

"I'm glad you came around," Taylor told Bryant as they put the shovels and snow blower in the garage. "You really surprised me."

"I just needed a little time to get used to the idea of Mom dating," Bryant responded.

"Good, because she likes Deacon Hampton."

"I know. So, who are you seeing now that you and Jennifer are done for good?"

"No one," Taylor answered then grinned. "I'm waiting until after Christmas and Valentine's Day to start dating again."

They closed the garage and went inside.

Later that day, Bryant surprised Taylor again. During holiday dinners, Bryant was used to sitting at the opposite end of the table from his mother, who sat at the head of the table. But this afternoon, when the family walked in the dining room, Bryant offered the chair at the opposite end of the table to his mother's guest, Deacon Hampton. Then he went and sat at the extra place setting on his mother's right. Samantha sat between Bryant and Kyle, and Kyle Jr. sat in a highchair between his parents. Talia sat on the other side of the table between Taylor and her new boyfriend, Lawrence. The other extra place setting was for him. When everyone was seated, Bryant said the grace. Taylor looked across the table at Bryant and nodded, signaling his approval.

That evening, Bryant and Taylor went to the theater to catch a new action comedy starring comedian Kevin Hart. Afterwards, they stopped by Talia's apartment and had a few drinks with her and Lawrence. Jennifer moved after she and Taylor broke up because she said it would be too hard getting over him when he was at the apartment all the time visiting his sister. Talia turned Jennifer's old bedroom into a guest room and that's where Bryant and Taylor ended up sleeping after having two too many drinks.

Bryant woke Taylor up bright and early the next morning. They knocked on Talia's bedroom door and told her they were leaving so Bryant could pack and get ready for his flight back to Atlanta. Felicia was preparing breakfast when they arrived at the house. Bryant went upstairs and started packing, while Taylor sat in the kitchen and drank a cup of coffee. As Bryant packed his suitcase, he began thinking about next Christmas and wondering – after Cassie didn't show up at the café, if it was time to move on. He put his life on hold to wait for her two years ago. She married another man while he was waiting, and he could only assume that she was happily married since she didn't show up at the café. He asked himself – out loud so he was sure he heard, "How long are you going to keep waiting?" When he was done packing, he carried his suitcase and bag downstairs. Felicia and Taylor were already in the dining room. "I was about to get started without you," Taylor said. Bryant sat down then he and Taylor began eating. Felicia sat at the table sipping a cup of coffee and smiling as she watched her sons devour the meal she prepared for them.

An hour later, Bryant and Taylor carried Bryant's luggage out to the car. Felicia followed them. She asked Bryant, "When can we expect to see you again?"

"I'll have some vacation time next year, but I'm not sure when I'll use it. Whenever I come, I'll be able to stay for more than a couple of days," Bryant told his mother before he kissed her and got in Taylor's Mustang. "I'll call you when I get home."

Taylor backed out the driveway. "I love you," Felicia yelled as he pulled onto the street. "Both of you!" Taylor responded by tapping the car horn twice.

The snow and ice had melted, so the neighborhood streets were clear. When they came to the main highway, Taylor turned on the entrance ramp then merged into traffic on the highway.

Bryant's flight was at 3:30. He looked at his watch. It was 12:22. That meant he had time to stop by the café. "When you get to the Malloy Street exit, take it. I want to stop by the café before I go."

"Do we have time?" Taylor asked.

"It's just 12:22, and my flight's at 3:30."

"Well, you can't get in there and go on and on like you do."

"I just want to say bye."

"Yeah, say bye and ask did Cassie come after you left." Taylor looked over at Bryant and grinned. "I may be the younger brother, but..."

"Watch it!" Bryant yelled.

Taylor turned just in time to see the cars in front of him slowing to a stop. He mashed the brakes and the car skidded to within a few inches of the car in front of him. It took a second for both of them to exhale and relax. "Damn that was close," Taylor said. They both looked at the line of cars ahead of them but could not see where the stalled traffic began.

"I wonder what's happened?" Bryant asked.

"Ain't no telling. Could be an accident. Could be them working on the road. They're always out here working on the highway, but I never see anything they've done."

Bryant looked at his watch. It was 12:24.

Ten minutes later, they were still sitting in the same spot.

At 12:41, the traffic started moving slowly. After they drove about forty yards, traffic stalled again, then stopped.

Bryant glanced nervously at his watch. "If this traffic doesn't..."

"Stop," Taylor cut him off. "Don't say it or you'll jinx us."

Seventeen minutes later, traffic started moving again.

Fourteen minutes and nearly a mile later, traffic was directed into a single lane to allow cars to pass safely by a charred car that a team of firemen had just extinguished.

"I don't think you're going to have time to go by the café," Taylor said as they drove past the burnt car.

Bryant looked at his watch. It was 1:28. "I don't think so either," he said. "It's the holidays and the lines at the security checkpoints are going to be long, so take me to the airport."

Two hours later, Bryant was staring out the window of an airplane as it sped down the runway then propelled itself into the sky for a flight to Atlanta.

The Year
After That

Chapter 29

The new year brought more changes to Cassie's life. She had gotten divorced from Malcolm and entered the new year free of the anger and hurt caused by his betrayal. After spending the past eight months living with her parents, she was ready to move into her own place. She needed to be home with them after she left Malcolm. Her spirit was broken, along with her heart. She felt humiliated and disgraced. And, she was angry. Angry with him for moving her to Chicago so he could continue his affair in Memphis when he flew back for work. Angry with herself for moving to Chicago and marrying him after she had caught him cheating. Finally, the anger was gone, and the hurt had become a bad memory that her maimed heart forced her to remember instead of letting her discard it.

She found a small house a few blocks from the hospital, where she had been working since September. The cottage-style house was inviting with its large windows and front porch swing. Cassie moved in the second week of January. The day she moved in was exactly three weeks after she flew to Chicago on Christmas Eve in hopes of meeting Bryant at Pearlie Mae's Café. Her mother was still talking about the results of that trip the day she helped Cassie unpack some things in the bedroom of the new house.

"I chickened out," Cassie explained again as she walked in the closet with an armload of dresses on hangers. She hung the dresses on the left side of the closet.

"But how could you after all your talk about him being the perfect man?" Margaret asked while straightening the curtains in the bedroom.

"He is," Cassie said, walking out of the closet. "Like I told you before, I was parking when I saw him in the café sitting in our booth. I opened the car door to get out, but I couldn't."

"So, you flew all the way to Chicago on Christmas Eve just to sit in the car in front of the cafe?"

"I wasn't ready, and I didn't want to show up looking like someone he needed to save again," Cassie answered. "So yes. I flew all the way to Chicago on Christmas Eve and just sat in the car watching him wait for me. And it was so worth it."

"I'm sure it was," Margaret responded. "After all, on a scale of zero to one-hundred, he gets a gazillion points for showing up every year."

It was Margaret who convinced Cassie to fly to Chicago on Christmas Eve to meet up with Bryant. When Cassie returned to Memphis two hours after midnight and told her mother what had happened, Margaret was a little disappointed that they had not gotten together, but she was happy knowing that Bryant, a man she had yet to meet, was helping her daughter's heart heal.

The previous July, the day after Cassie and Darryl returned from Chicago, Cassie filed for divorce. The next day, while she and her mother were at the nail salon getting manicures and pedicures, Cassie told Margaret about Bryant and how they met. She started by finally telling the truth – that the accident occurred after Malcolm told her his flight was cancelled and he wasn't going to make it home on Christmas Eve. She had left that part out during her earlier recounting to her parents. "I caught him with Anita about a year before we moved to Chicago," Cassie revealed. "And when he said he couldn't make it home, I automatically assumed it was because he was with her. That's why I wasn't paying attention and ran the stoplight."

"Why are you just now telling me this?" asked Margaret, the dismay showing on her face. "And, why did you move with him to Chicago and then marry him after you caught him cheating?"

"Because I loved him, Mom," Cassie admitted. "And, I thought once we moved to Chicago, whatever he had with her would be over." Cassie shook her head no. "Mom, I really don't want to talk about Malcolm. I only mentioned him and the accident to get to how I met Bryant."

Before they left the nail salon, Cassie told Margaret everything she could remember about Bryant. She explained how Bryant followed her into the café, sat across from her in the booth, and just started talking. Her face lit up when she described the wonderful time they had at Macy's shopping for Christmas presents to replace the gift cards he had gotten for his family. She smiled reminiscently as she recalled him saying she was beautiful, then the thought of him kissing her under the mistletoe caused her to blush.

"When I spoke to you on the phone Christmas morning, I wanted to tell you so badly about how I had met the most perfect guy the day before, but I decided not to," Cassie said as they walked out the nail salon to her car.

"And why was that?" Margaret asked. She got in the car on the passenger side.

"Because we had just sent out all those wedding invitations, and I didn't want you chasing the mail truck all over the city trying to retrieve them."

"You know I would've," Margaret concurred.

When they made it home, Cassie turned on her laptop then went to Bryant's Facebook page. She strolled down to his December posts and stopped on the photo of Bryant, Mabel, and Jake at the café on Christmas Eve. She picked up the laptop and walked out her bedroom and downstairs to the den, where Margaret was watching television.

"Mom, I want to show you something," she said and sat the laptop on the table in front of her mother. "This is Bryant. He took this picture at the café Christmas Eve."

Margaret looked at the photo of Bryant, Mabel, and Jake. "I assume you're talking about the handsome young man and not the handsome older man who could be your grandfather."

"That's Mr. Jake. He owns the café. And that's Mrs. Mabel," Cassie pointed out. "Bryant said he would be at the café on Christmas Eve waiting for me, and he was there."

From that moment on, Margaret was Bryant's biggest cheerleader. She even bought the round-trip tickets from Memphis to Chicago for Cassie to try and meet Bryant at the café on Christmas Eve. Margaret understood – her daughter was mending, still healing, but she wasn't giving up. She wanted Cassie with Bryant. That is why she was still talking about it the second Saturday in January when she helped Cassie move into the two-bedroom, cottage-style house near the hospital.

Cassie and Margaret were in the kitchen unpacking boxes of dishes and placing them in the cabinet. "I still think you should reach out to Bryant," Margaret said. Before Cassie could answer, Margaret suggested, "You may not be ready to meet him face to face right now, but you can call him."

"I don't have his phone number," Cassie responded.

"Then send him a friend request on Facebook."

Cassie turned to her mother. "Mom, I can't just go barging into his life. What if he's seeing someone?"

Margaret stopped putting the dishes up and walked up to Cassie. "I don't think he would've spent the last two Christmas Eves waiting on you at that café if he was seeing someone else."

"You may be right, but I still can't," Cassie said. "Not right now."

Margaret shook her head, "I understand. Take your time, and don't let me rush you."

"Thanks, Mom," Cassie said and hugged her mother. "I love you."

"I love you, too," Margaret responded.

Nathaniel walked in the kitchen and saw them embracing. "What's going on?"

"We were just having a moment," Margaret told him.

Later, Cassie and Margaret ordered Chinese food, then they enjoyed dinner with Nathaniel, Darryl, and a friend of Darryl's, who spent his Saturday helping her move. It was around 9:30 when they all left. Once she was alone in the house, Cassie walked from room to room, outside on the porch, then back in the living room. It felt good to be in her own place and to see her new life taking shape. She was so full of joy and pride that first night she could hardly sleep.

Chapter 30

Breathe in. Breathe out. Bryant stood on his bedroom's balcony reminding himself how to breathe. Breathe in then breathe out. Breathe in. Breathe out. Breathe in. Breathe out. In then out.

The sky was dark and starless, finite like the sky inside of a snow globe. It was quiet – the only noise louder than his dizzying thoughts was the wheezing sound he made as he gasped for air. The air was frigid and still.

Breathe in. Breathe out. Breathe in. Breathe out.

Bryant had gone to bed around 10:30. He slept soundly for a couple of hours, and then, without warning, a crushing feeling of dread jarred him awake. He sprang to his feet. He couldn't breathe. His mind was racing – thinking a hundred thoughts simultaneously, but none clear enough to understand. He could feel the tension gripping his chest, tightening across his body. He stumbled toward the balcony then struggled to unlock and open the door. As soon as he stepped on the balcony, he willed himself to, "Breathe in. Breathe out. Breathe in. Breathe out."

Being able to breathe calmed him. He could feel the tension relaxing its grip on his body. His mind slowed enough for him to realize the hundred thoughts were really one thought – one question ricocheting back and forth because he could not answer it. Is it time to move on? That question had been on his mind since Christmas morning when he realized he had spent the past two years with his personal life on hold waiting and hoping she would walk back into his life even though she was married. As soon as he gave up and told himself that he would never see her again, that she would never be his, an overwhelming feeling of loss engulfed him like a gelatinous cloud that morning. He thought he would be able to shake it off when he made it back to Atlanta, but that didn't happen. He had been back in Atlanta two weeks, and during those two weeks, he'd woken up three times in the middle of the night feeling like he was suffocating – choking on the truth, which made it hard to breathe.

The January night air was starting to feel even colder. His teeth chattered as the spiteful wind swept across the balcony. Bryant took a deep breath then exhaled before going inside. After closing and locking the balcony door, he walked out the bedroom into the living room and sat at his desk. He stared at Cassie's wedding picture and wondered aloud, "How did I let myself fall when I knew you were marrying someone else?" Bryant picked up the framed picture. "I wish I could talk to you, so I can make you understand why I have to renege on my word. I thought that I could wait for you, but I realize now that life won't wait with me. While I've been waiting, you've married and gone on with your life. And my family – Mom, Taylor, Samantha, Talia, they're going on with their lives. I'm happy for them, and I want to be happy for you. I can't keep waiting Cassie. I can't."

It was a week into the new year, and he had not made a New Year's resolution yet. He knew what his resolution was going to be when the new year came in, but he was in no rush to make it because he usually stuck to his resolutions and did what he set out to do. Now was the time to make his resolution. Now, after waking up in the middle of an anxiety attack triggered by the question he was trying not to answer. Is it time to move on?

He opened the desk drawer.

"I resolve to move on with my life this year," he said and put Cassie's wedding picture inside the drawer. "I resolve to be happy this year – to be happy even if it's not with you." Then he put the framed selfie of him and Cassie in the drawer.

He closed the desk drawer. Then, he sat there and thought about what he needed to do next to prove Cassie was out of his life and he was moving on. "Rhena," he suggested aloud to himself. "Why don't you call Rhena?"

"That's what I'll do," he responded. "I'll call Rhena." He looked at the clock above the desk. "It's too late, so I'll call her in the morning."

When the alarm clock rang four hours later, Bryant knocked the clock off the bedside table trying to press the snooze button. He leaned over the side of the bed and turned off the alarm clock then put it back on the table. He sat up on the side of the bed and looked past the balcony at the cloudless sky. Fifty-three minutes later, after taking a shower, getting dressed for work, and starting toward the front door, he turned around and walked over to his desk. He opened the drawer, removed Cassie's framed wedding photo and their framed selfie, and then placed them in the same spots they had occupied on the desk. Calling Rhena didn't cross his mind.

Perhaps, the biggest change the new year brought for Bryant – and the way he appeased his desire for something to be moving forward in his life – was his decision to move closer to his job in Dunwoody. He was tired of the daily commute from his apartment in Marietta to his job at the Journal Constitution, and he felt he was spending more time in his car than he was spending waking hours at his apartment. So, in mid-February, he packed his belongings in a U-Haul and moved them to a two-bedroom house on a cul-de-sac in a modest Dunwoody neighborhood. From the outside, the two-floor house looked smaller than it was. The bedrooms, both upstairs, were spacious, and each had its own bathroom. The living room and kitchen were large enough, but the dining room could have been a tad bigger.

The house had a den that he turned into an office, where he spent most of the little free time he had. Cassie's framed wedding photo and their framed selfie still sat on his desk.

After breaking his New Year's resolution a few hours after making it, Bryant wasn't sure which side of the fence he was on when it came to Cassie. Was he still holding on or was he in the process of letting go? Despite not knowing the answer to this question, he made sure he kept his Facebook page regularly updated about whatever was going on in his life in case she ever visited his page. He had no way of knowing what was going on in her life, but he imagined that every now and then she slipped away from Malcolm to spend time browsing through his Facebook posts to see what he had been up to. The day he moved into the house in Dunwoody, he made sure he took several pictures that he could post.

Cal was helping him carry a sofa into the living room when Bryant stopped to pose for a picture. "What are you doing?" Cal asked.

"John's taking a picture for me," Bryant answered.

John moved away from the living room window to get a clearer shot.

"What's taking you so long?" Cal asked John.

"I'm trying to get a better shot," John replied. "Are you ready, Bryant?"

"Yeah," he answered and smiled for the camera.

John took four shots back to back. "I hope I got one or two good ones," he said and started reviewing the pictures. Bryant sat his end of the sofa down to look at the pictures, leaving Cal still standing in the doorway holding up his end of the sofa. Cal put his end down and dived on the sofa.

"What are you doing?" Bryant asked.

"I'm through, and when you find time to bring the sofa on in, I'm not moving," Cal said and got comfortable on the sofa. Bryant and John had to move the sofa to its place in the living room with Cal lying on it.

Later that night, while eating pizza and wings, drinking a few beers, and watching the University of Florida best Villanova in a men's basketball game, Cal told Bryant he needed a favor. "What's that?" Bryant asked.

"My girl's cousin will be visiting next weekend, and I want you to go out with us," Cal answered.

Before Bryant could respond, John blurted, "Didn't I tell you he was going to say no unless your girl cousin's name is Cassie...Hold on. I can't remember her last name. Or did I ever know it?"

"Damn you," Bryant said and gave John the finger.

"She's your type," Cal continued. "Smart. Pretty. Fine. I'm telling you man, she's hot."

"Have you met her?" John asked.

"No," Cal answered. "But Michelle says she is." He waited for Bryant to respond. After he didn't, Cal pressed for an answer, "Well?"

"Let me see what my schedule's like next week, and I'll let you know," Bryant answered.

"He didn't say go out with them next week," John interjected. "He said next weekend."

"I know what he said," Bryant responded. "Cal, I'll let you know."

John put down his beer then turned to Bryant. "Man, I have to ask. I know it ain't my business, but for some damn reason, I just want to know."

"Know what?"

"When was the last time you got laid?" John asked. "I mean, you met this Cassie over two years ago and I haven't heard you mention another woman since. Makes me wonder."

"Me too," Cal added. "What's up man? Two years is a long time to be celibate."

Bryant grinned and shook his head. "What y'all hatin' asses need to do is get out of my business," he said.

"We're just trying to help," John said, trying not to laugh. "I mean, we were about to put our quarters together and call Rent-A-Woman for you."

Cal laughed out loud. So, did Bryant.

After the game ended and Cal and John headed home to Marietta, Bryant sat at his desk and posted the pictures he had taken that day on his Facebook page and captioned them, "Moving in…" His mother was the first person to like the post and to comment. "Get my room ready," she wrote.

The next day, Bryant called Cal and told him he would be spending next weekend with a young swimmer, an Olympic hopeful, he was profiling for a freelance writing assignment, so he couldn't accept the invitation to go out with Michelle's cousin.

Chapter 31

Bryant landed a freelance job chasing dreams. Not his own, at least not at first.

In February, right before he moved to Dunwoody, Bryant's supervising editor, Sheila, at the Journal Constitution recommended him to a former colleague who was the editor of an Atlanta-based national lifestyle magazine, *Soar*. He landed the assignment to write a series of personality profiles of people chasing their personal dreams starting with the May issue. His first profile was of a record-setting high school swimmer chasing his dream of competing in the Summer Olympics.

Bryant's mom called after she bought the magazine and read his article about the high school swimmer. She could hardly contain her excitement. "I had to go to two Walmart stores to find six copies of the magazine, so I can give Samantha, Talia, Taylor and Hamp a copy and I can keep two. Do I need to get another copy and send you?" She laughed. "I'm just teasing. I just had to call and let you know that I am so proud of you."

"I am too," Taylor, who was sitting in the living room with his mother, yelled.

"Thanks, Mom, and tell Taylor I said thanks."

"You're on speaker, so he heard you," Felicia replied.

"Did Mom tell you about the new car?" Taylor asked.

"No, I haven't," Felicia answered before Bryant could respond. "But since you brought it up, I will. And, I'm going to tell him how you've started speeding and driving like a maniac since you got it."

"What kind of car did you get?"

"A new metallic Lexus RC," Taylor answered.

"I guess that's what a six-figure income buys you," Bryant said. "Congrats man."

"Give me a year or two, and I'll be at seven-figures," Taylor replied.

"That's when I'm coming to work for you."

The next day, after he got in from work, Samantha called to congratulate him.

It was two days later when Taylor saw Talia and gave her the magazine. She called Bryant that same day and told him she gave the article a thumbs up.

The swimmer profile was followed by a profile of a mother and housewife who turned her dream of starting a parenting magazine into a children and parenting media empire. Bryant enjoyed working on the personality profiles because the stories required him to spend time with the people being profiled. He got to hang in the studio and watch and listen as an aspiring composer created music for his first movie soundtrack. And, he got to be a taste tester when he profiled a young chef who was opening his own Caribbean restaurant.

Writing about other people chasing their dreams motivated Bryant to chase his own dreams. He finally opened the screenwriting software Taylor gave him for Christmas and started writing his first screenplay – a suspense thriller, *The Lost Day*, about a reporter uncovering a twenty-year-old mystery. He even enrolled in a screenwriting course at the Film Institute. That's where he met Victor Maldonado.

Bryant knew the name Victor Maldonado before he met the man the name belonged to. The screenwriting class was from 6 p.m. to 9 p.m. on Tuesdays and Thursdays. At the beginning of the first class, the instructor did a roll call. Fifteen of the sixteen students enrolled in the course were present. Victor Maldonado wasn't. The instructor, Professor Jack Franklin, called Victor's full name twice, then his first name again, before he concluded, "I guess Mister Maldonado isn't joining us tonight." At the beginning of Thursday evening's class, Professor Franklin called the roll. Again, fifteen of the sixteen students were present. This time, he called Victor's first name once and glanced over his spectacles to see if Victor was sitting in the class but did not hear his name called. "I guess Mister Maldonado won't be joining us tonight," he told the class.

The following Tuesday, Bryant was sitting at a table on the front row of the classroom when Professor Franklin called the roll. "Victor Maldonado," he called and visually scanned the classroom.

"I'm here," a voice in the back replied.

Bryant glanced back to see a guy about his age enter the classroom.

"Sorry, I'm late," the guy said and walked up to the front table where Bryant was sitting. He looked to be in his early thirties, was about Bryant's size and height, but with more of an athletic build. He appeared to be sharp, hip, and maybe even artistic, but he didn't look like a writer, at least not to Bryant. "Excuse me," he said. "Is anyone sitting here?"

"No," Bryant responded.

Victor sat down.

"It's a good thing you showed up tonight, Mr. Maldonado," Professor Franklin said. "I was about to have you dropped from the course. It's a ten-week course, and you missed the entire first week."

"It was my fault," Victor responded. "I…"

Professor Franklin cut him off. "I'm sure you did," he joked. "It's good to have you here Mr. Maldonado. Maybe Mr. Fuller will give you a recap of last week's assignment…after class."

Bryant looked at Victor and said, "Sure."

As they walked toward the parking lot after class, Bryant told Victor the assignment Professor Franklin had given the class last week was due at the beginning of class Thursday and that the directions for the assignment were in the course syllabus. "I don't think you'll have any problems with it," Bryant said as he started toward his car. He glanced back and noticed Victor had stopped on the sidewalk. "Is everything okay?" Bryant asked.

"Yeah," Victor answered. "My car's in the shop, so my fiancée is picking me up. I was on my way here last Tuesday when it put me down."

"Well, I'll see you Thursday," Bryant said and pressed the unlock button on his keychain. Bryant glanced in his rearview mirror as he was driving out of the parking lot and saw a black car pull up and stop in front of Victor.

Thursday, when Bryant walked in the classroom, Victor was already seated at the table on the front row. Bryant sat in the other chair at the table. "How's it going?" Bryant asked.

"I can't complain," Victor responded. "Well, yes I can, but I guess I shouldn't."

"How did the assignment go?" Bryant inquired.

"It was pretty straightforward," Victor answered. "I think I may have a knack for screenwriting."

"If you don't mind me asking, what's your day job?" Bryant asked.

"I'm a film and video editor for an advertising production company," Victor responded. "I've always dreamed of writing and directing my own projects, and I guess I've talked about it so much that my fiancée enrolled me in writing and directing courses here as an engagement present."

"Wow! Talk about a good gift giver." Bryant was about to ask Victor about his fiancée when Professor Franklin walked in the classroom. As Professor Franklin greeted the students, Bryant's thoughts fell on Cassie, who was a good gift giver.

Later, after Bryant waved goodbye to Victor and started toward his car, he saw the black car pull up to the sidewalk and stop in front of Victor.

"Bryant!" Victor yelled across the parking lot. "Bryant!" When Bryant turned around, Victor said, "I want you to meet my fiancée."

Bryant was walking toward Victor when the driver's door of the black car opened and Rhena got out the car. Bryant stopped him his tracks. When Rhena turned and saw Bryant, she was visibly surprised. "You two know each other?" Victor asked.

"This is Bryant...the guy I told you about," Rhena answered.

"Your ex Bryant?" Victor inquired.

"He wasn't really my ex," she answered. "We went out on a few dates, but he broke it off."

Victor remembered her telling him, "For a woman he..."

"Victor!" Rhena cut him off. She looked at Bryant. "I'm sorry."

"No problem," Bryant responded.

Victor walked around the car, put his arms around Rhena, and told her, "Baby, I told him we're getting married."

"Congratulations," Bryant said.

"Thank you," Rhena and Victor both replied.

"Well, I need to be going," Bryant said as soon as he sensed the awkwardness of the moment. "It was nice seeing you again."

"You too," Rhena responded.

"See you in class next week," Victor said as Bryant walked away.

Bryant tried to take his time walking to his car and driving off, but he was in a hurry to leave – to get away before Rhena and Victor saw how unhappy their happiness made him. Bryant wasn't upset because Rhena was getting married, but her getting married made him envious. He was still pining for a woman whose last name he didn't even know, while Rhena, a woman who could have been his, had found someone else. As he drove home, he became angry with Cassie for not being with him and angry with himself for falling for her in the first place.

When he got home, he walked over to the desk and put Cassie's wedding photo and their selfie in the desk drawer. Then he sat down, turned on the computer, and deactivated his Facebook page. The next morning, Bryant woke up wondering what the odds were that of the hundreds of thousands of men in Atlanta, the man that was about to marry the last woman he dated would walk into a screenwriting class and sit down next to him. He wondered how he would feel talking, working, and laughing with Victor now that he knew about Rhena. He didn't wonder long. Bryant went online and withdrew from the course. He decided he would wait until the fall or spring semester to take the course.

Chapter 32

Bryant loved his house, especially when the holiday season rolled around, and he had a yard he could decorate. The past four years, he'd lived in an apartment and was restricted to only decorating the inside of the apartment and placing a small wreathe on the door. Before he moved to Atlanta, he was responsible for decorating his mother's yard, a task he started doing as a child with his father. When Taylor was old enough, he joined them. After he moved – and didn't make it back home until a day or two before Christmas, Taylor took over decorating their mother's yard. Bryant had been looking forward to decorating his yard since he moved in the house, so he began shopping for Christmas decorations in September, as soon as the stores put them on the shelves. He decided to get rid of his old Christmas decorations, except for the keepsake ornaments, so the closet in the den was packed with new lights, ornaments, and assorted decor. He was ready for Thanksgiving to come and then go, so he could get to work.

John and his wife, Lacey, invited Bryant over for Thanksgiving, so he spent most of the day at their house in Marietta. Bryant, to his surprise, finally ended up meeting Cal's girl's cousin, Beverly, when Cal and Michelle brought her with them to John's house for Thanksgiving dinner. Michelle's description of her cousin had been on target. Cal nudged Bryant and pointed out, "Pretty, isn't she?"

"She's beautiful," Bryant agreed.

"Smart too," Cal added. "She's about to move here and open her own law practice."

Beverly and Michelle saw Cal whispering to Bryant and they both knew what he was up too. "Let me cut to the chase," Michelle told Beverly. They walked over to the bar, where Cal was pouring him and Bryant a shot of Maker's Mark Bourbon. "Bryant," Michelle said. "I want to introduce you to my cousin Beverly."

"Hi Beverly," he responded. "I'm Bryant, Cal's buddy."

"Please stop saying that like it's an endorsement," Michelle quipped. "Cal, can I talk to you in the dining room?"

"Sure," Cal replied. He handed Bryant a shot glass and winked. "Drink you a few more of these, and you'll be okay." Then he followed Michelle into the dining room.

Bryant spent the next hour talking with Beverly. They talked about her moving from Tallahassee to Atlanta to open her law practice. They talked about his job at the Journal Constitution and his series with *Soar* magazine. He talked about growing up in Chicago and moving to Atlanta. She talked about growing up in Tallahassee and her upcoming move to Atlanta. By the time, they ran out of things to talk about, John and Lacey called everyone into the dining room. After dinner, Bryant and the fellows flipped back and forth between a couple of football games on television. Then they took the bottle of Maker's Mark, a couple of shot glasses, and a marijuana blunt Cal had rolled and went out back for an hour or so. When they came back in, Bryant told John and Lacey he needed to leave because he had to get up early the next morning. Before leaving though, he walked over to Beverly and told her he hoped to see her when she returned for Christmas. Lacey overheard him. "Bryant, I forgot John said you were staying in Atlanta for Christmas," Lacey said. "So, I'm giving you your invitation for Christmas dinner now."

"I'll be here," he told Lacey.

Bryant woke up before sunrise ready to kickstart the Christmas season. As he drove toward the mall, he smiled thinking about his transformation from a man who hated shopping so bad that he bought everyone gift cards to a man who was up before dawn, ready to shop, on Black Friday. He credited his time with Cassie for his transformation. Bryant spent about three hours browsing through stores until he found all the presents that he wanted for everyone on his Christmas list. He figured Jake had stashed the gift he left for Cassie in his office desk, so there was no need for him to buy and ship another gift to Jake that she would never receive. When he made it home, he wrapped all the gifts for his family then placed them in a box for shipment to Chicago. Before he went to bed, he pulled the box with the new pre-lit Christmas tree into the living room and stacked the new decorations and the boxes containing the keepsake ornaments in a corner.

The next morning, the Saturday after Thanksgiving, he woke up around seven. He ate two warmed Krispy Kreme doughnuts and drank a cup of coffee for breakfast. He spent the rest of the morning decorating his Christmas tree and living room in a fall foliage theme. He placed the wrapped presents for John and his family, Cal, and his editor, Sheila, under the tree. When he was done inside, he carried the bags and boxes of exterior decorations out to the porch, where he separated and organized everything. He started by trimming the exterior of the house in multicolor lights. Then he placed nets of colorful lights across the hedges. He set two reindeer covered in clear lights in the middle of the yard. He was about to turn the lights on to make sure everything was properly connected when his cell phone rang. He looked at the caller id. It was Taylor calling. "What's up?" he answered the phone.

"It's Taylor."

"I know who it is. I recognize your voice, and your name popped up on my phone. What's going on?"

Taylor hesitated.

"Taylor?"

"I went over to Northwood Plaza today to do a little Christmas shopping," Taylor spoke slowly. "On the way home, I was driving past Pearlie Mae's and decided to stop and grab a cheeseburger." Taylor paused and considered how to say the rest of what he called to tell Bryant.

"And?" Bryant pushed him to continue.

"And I went inside and placed my order. While I was waiting on the order, I asked the waitress if Mr. Jake was there. And she told me Mr. Jake had..." he trailed off.

"What did you say?" Bryant sat on the steps. "Taylor?"

"She said he died a week before Thanksgiving."

Bryant felt his heart drop. "What happened?" he asked.

"She said, Mr. Jake's sister and his niece, Shirley, went to his house to pick him up for church and when they got there, he had gotten dressed and died sitting in a rocking chair on the porch. Shirley said he told her and her momma that he was ready to go see Mrs. Pearlie Mae a few days before he died. He said she was waiting on him."

Bryant couldn't believe what he was hearing.

"You okay?" Taylor asked.

"Yes," Bryant replied. "It's just that..." He couldn't put what he was feeling into words.

"I know," Taylor said. "It's sad."

"I wonder what's going to happen to the café," Bryant thought out loud.

"The waitress said Shirley runs the café now."

Later, after hanging up with Taylor, Bryant sat at his desk and thought about Jake, his wife Pearlie Mae, and the cafe. Having spent the past three Christmas Eves listening to Jake talk about his wife, he knew how much Jake loved her and how the café kept her present in his life even after she passed. It was easy for Bryant to believe that Jake woke up one Sunday morning, got dressed for church, sat in a rocking chair on the porch, and rocked his way home to be with Pearlie Mae. Thinking about the café brought

Cassie back front and center in his mind. He took her framed wedding photo and their framed selfie photo out the desk drawer, where they had been since the night he found out Rhena was marrying Victor from the screenwriting class. After waiting for Cassie at the café last Christmas Eve, he started to see the pointlessness of waiting for a woman he met and hung out with a few hours to leave a man she married and come back to him. The more he thought about it, the more illogical it seemed. He still thought she was perfect for him, but the reality was she had a life with someone else. He had to accept this, so he did. He decided to stay in Atlanta to make sure he didn't spend Christmas Eve at the café waiting for someone who was not going to show up. He placed both photos back in the drawer.

Chapter 33

Bryant's day was feeling a bit off. He knew it was going to be an atypical day because it was two days before Christmas, he was off from work, and he was preparing to spend his first Christmas in Atlanta – away from home – and he already missed being there with his mom and family. But the uneasy feeling that he'd felt all that day was something else. His day didn't start out quite right because he slept through the 6:30 alarm that he turns off every morning before it rings. But, not this morning. He slept through the alarm and only woke up – forty-five minutes later – because he had to use the bathroom. He felt the uneasiness weighing down on him as he teetered toward the bathroom. At first, he thought the peculiar feeling had something to do with not being at the café waiting for Cassie like he told her he would every Christmas Eve. Tomorrow was Christmas Eve, and he was going to be over eight-hundred miles away from the café. During the past few months, Bryant managed to make Cassie a passing daily thought, but he knew the closer it got to Christmas Eve, the more she would monopolize his day.

Bryant showered and slipped on a pair of blue lounging pants and a matching long-sleeved shirt. He went into the kitchen and put on a pot of coffee. While the coffee was brewing, he sat on a stool and said out loud so he would be sure he heard himself, "You're doing the right thing by staying in Atlanta for Christmas and…" He hesitated before saying, "…and not waiting for her at the café." Bryant knew that the only way for him to not be at the café on Christmas Eve waiting for her was for him to stay in Atlanta. He poured a cup of coffee then went into the living room and sat in a chair by the window.

A light frost covered the ground, which reminded him of home, where most Christmases were white. The sky was overcast, and the temperature outside looked to be in the low twenties, like the weather forecast had predicted. He wasn't home, but at least it looked and felt like Christmas from where he was sitting. Bryant knew the frost would not remain on the ground past mid-morning, but he still hoped it would. The frost didn't last until mid-morning. An hour later, it was gone. Bryant was walking past the window when he looked outside and saw that the wind had knocked over one of the lighted reindeer in the yard. Before going out in the cold to straighten the reindeer and the other decoration, Bryant dressed for the weather – a sweater, coat, a pair of jeans over thermal underwear, boots, and a wool beanie. As he placed the reindeer in an upright position, he remembered Taylor calling to tell him Mr. Jake had died. It was the Saturday after Thanksgiving, and he was in the yard putting up the Christmas lights and decoration. He already knew he wasn't going home for Christmas but hearing Mr. Jake had passed made him want to change his mind. If he had gone to Chicago, he would have stopped by the café to show his respect to Mr. Jake's niece Shirley and to find out how Mrs. Mabel was doing. And going to the café would not have had anything to do with Cassie, he told himself as he stood the reindeer back up.

The day was passing slower than usual. By noon, he had cleaned the house, washed and dried a load of clothes, and watched a Christmas movie on Netflix. He fought the urge to call his mother, Taylor, or his sisters back home. He figured talking to them would make him want to be there with them. He was pacing back and forth through the house trying to figure out what to do next, when he thought about the screenplay he started writing during the summer. He worked on the screenplay for about a week after he dropped out the screenwriting course. He had not looked at it since. Bryant sat at his desk, turned on the laptop, then opened the file labeled, "The Lost Day – A Screenplay." Bryant was surprised when he saw the document was twenty-two pages. He didn't think he had gotten that far with the suspense thriller. Bryant was reading the screenplay to refresh his memory when his phone rang. He looked at the phone and saw it was Talia calling. He pressed the answer and speaker keys. "Talk to me," he said.

"You need to hurry home," Talia screamed. "Taylor's been in a bad car wreck, and he's hurt really bad!"

"Taylor's been in a wreck?"

"He lost control of the car on the freeway then crashed and overturned. He's hurt bad," Talia cried. "We need you here, Bryant! Come home! Hurry!"

"I'm checking for a flight now!"

Bryant went online and found a flight that was leaving Atlanta for Chicago at 5:45 and booked it. He gave Talia the flight information so she could pick him up from O'Hare in Chicago. After he hung up the phone with Talia, he called Cal and John to tell them he had to hurry home because Taylor had been in an accident. Cal offered to drive him to the airport. Bryant rushed to pack a small suitcase and to get dressed before Cal arrived.

As Cal drove to the airport, Bryant called Talia to find out how Taylor was doing.

"He's in surgery," Talia informed him. "He has some broken ribs and a collapsed lung so that had to take him into surgery right away. And, we're just waiting." She sniffed, trying to stop the tears. "He also has a broken arm and a gash on his head that required several stitches."

Bryant wished he were already there with his brother and family. "Is Mom still with you?" he asked. He struggled to keep his composure.

"Yes, she's right here," Talia answered.

"How is she?"

"She was really upset, but Samantha and Deacon Hampton calmed her down," Talia answered.

"Let her know that I'm on my way to the airport and I'll be there in a couple of hours," he said.

"I will," Talia replied. "I'll be at the airport to pick you up."

Before Bryant got out the car at the airport, he told Cal to let Michelle's cousin Beverly know he had to rush home to see about his brother.

"So, you like Bev?" Cal asked.

"It's not that." Bryant was about to elaborate. "Just tell her, okay."

"I'll let her know when she gets here tonight."

An hour and thirty-six minutes later, Bryant boarded a plane for Chicago. Talia and her boyfriend Lawrence were waiting at O'Hare International Airport when Bryant's flight arrived.

"How is he?" Bryant asked as soon as he got in the car.

"He's out of surgery," Talia answered. "But he hasn't regained consciousness."

"The doctors say the surgery went well," Lawrence added.

"Yeah," Talia confirmed. "Now, all we can do is wait."

Bryant watched Lawrence reach over and hold Talia's hand. "He'll pull through," Lawrence told her. She nodded in agreement then wiped her tears away with her other hand. Bryant turned and stared out the window at the highway. Snow had fallen the previous night, so the roads were still icy. He felt the road conditions contributed to Taylor's accident, which he surmised was the reason why his day had been feeling off.

Kyle had just made it back to the hospital after dropping Kyle Jr. off at his sister's house when Lawrence pulled in the parking space next to him. "Samantha just called and said they've moved him to the Intensive Care

Unit, and they're in the ICU waiting room.," Kyle said as they got out the cars.

"Did she say how he was doing?" Bryant asked.

"The doctor is coming out to speak to them in a few minutes," Kyle answered as they all started toward the hospital entrance.

Samantha, Felicia, and Deacon Hampton were in the ICU waiting room when the door opened, and Bryant rushed in and over to his mother. He flung his arms around her. Now that he was home with his family, with his mother's arms around him, he could no longer hold back his tears. "I'm sorry," he cried. "I should've been here."

"No," she responded and held him a little tighter. "You were where you were supposed to be. I'm just glad you're here now."

Chapter 34

Bryant spent the night sitting in a chair beside Taylor's bed in the intensive care unit. Samantha, Bryant, and Talia talked their mother into going home and getting some rest around midnight. Felicia didn't want to leave, and only agreed to go home after Bryant promised he would call her if there were any changes in Taylor's condition – good or bad. Talia and Lawrence followed Felicia and Deacon Hampton to the house and stayed with her until Samantha and Kyle arrived after picking Kyle Jr. up from Kyle's sister.

After they left for home, Bryant pulled the chair close to Taylor's bed and sat down. He had not been able to shake the guilt he felt when Talia called and told him about the accident. He leaned close to Taylor and told him, "I'm sorry, man. I should have been home, and none of this would've happened." Bryant thought about how he had woken up feeling like something was off about his day. Now, he knew what it was. He should've been in Chicago instead of trying to spend his first Christmas away from home. Bryant was still apologizing to Taylor when he received a text message from Samantha letting him know their mother had finally gone to bed. Then she asked if there were any changes with Taylor. He texted back and told her there were no changes and he would see them in the morning.

Bryant stared at Taylor, who looked like he was sleeping peacefully. The medical devices and tubes attached to him told a different story. The surgeon who operated on Taylor told the family that the surgery had gone well, and they were placing him in the intensive care unit for closer monitoring through the night. Each time Richard, the ICU nurse, came into the room to check on Taylor, he updated Bryant. Richard explained how Taylor's lung had collapsed and the air mask over his mouth and nose were helping him breathe and the tube extending from his chest was a drain to remove and prevent fluid buildup.

Bryant didn't get much sleep. He dozed off a few times, but as soon as Richard entered the room or one of the machines attached to Taylor beeped, he woke up. Around 6:30, Richard walked in the room with the day nurse, Brandy, which woke Bryant up. Richard introduced Brandy to Bryant before updating her on Taylor's condition and status. Bryant listened closely as he stared at his brother lying in bed.

"He's breathing much better than he was when they brought him in," Richard said. "And, his vitals are stabilizing."

Bryant was glad to hear this. "So, he's out of the woods?"

"I wouldn't say that just yet," Richard answered. "But he's doing a lot better."

As soon as Richard and Brandy walked out the room, Bryant's phone vibrated. He looked at the caller ID. It was Samantha. He answered, "Good morning."

"Mom's on her way to the hospital," Samantha said. "She was dressed and getting ready to leave when she woke me up. I tried to get her to wait for me, but you know your mother."

Bryant half-smiled. "Actually, I expected to see her walk through the door a couple of hours ago," he responded. "How long ago did she leave?"

"She just left," Samantha answered. "How's Taylor?"

"The nurse just said he was breathing much better than he was when they brought him into ICU and that his vitals were stabilizing," he answered.

"Thank God," Samantha said. "Well, I'm about to get dressed and come on to the hospital. Keep a lookout for Mom."

"I will," Bryant answered. "See you in a few." He pressed the key to end the call.

Bryant wanted to wash his face and freshen up before his mother arrived, so he went to the nurse station and asked Brandy where he could find a restroom. She told him there was one in the ICU waiting room. He walked out the intensive care unit into the hallway, where a large window framed the picturesque winter morning outside the hospital. He walked up to the window and gazed out. A light snow fell over the city. A small tractor plowed and salted the hospital's parking lot. The colorful lights on the 12-foot Christmas tree outside the main entrance glistened even after the gray morning clocked in and replaced the last remnants of the darkness. "Christmas Eve," he whispered loud enough for him to hear. "You're home, in Chicago, on Christmas Eve." He wouldn't allow himself to think the next thought. He walked away from the window and down the hallway to the waiting room.

Bryant was sitting in the ICU waiting room when he saw Felicia walking toward the intensive care unit. He hurried behind her. "Mom," he called as she pressed the button to speak with someone in the unit. She turned and saw Bryant walking up.

"May I help you?" a nurse asked over the speaker.

"I'm Taylor Fuller's mother and I would like to come in to see him," Felicia replied.

"Come on in," the nurse. The automatic doors opened.

"Samantha called," Bryant said. "I told her I expected you to be back a couple of hours ago."

"Taylor isn't like you and your sisters," she responded. "My baby needs me."

They walked inside.

"All your babies still need you," he said and put his arm around her.

Brandy was in the room checking on Taylor when Bryant and Felicia walked in. "How is he?" Felicia asked.

"His condition is improving," Brandy answered.

"Brandy, this is our mother, Felicia, and Mom, this is Brandy," Bryant introduced the two women.

"Brandy, thank you for taking such good care of my baby," Felicia said as she walked up to Taylor.

"You're welcome," Brandy replied. "If you need anything, I'll be at the station." Brandy started out the room.

Tears filled Felicia's eyes as she rubbed his face gently. "Good morning, Baby."

"Mom," Taylor mumbled through the breathing mask.

"Brandy!" Bryant shouted and rushed over to the bed. Brandy stopped in her tracks then hurried over to the bed. She took the breathing mask off Taylor.

"I'm right here," Felicia cried.

Taylor opened his eyes. "Bryant?" he asked, slightly confused.

"I'm right here," Bryant answered.

Taylor struggled trying to sit up. Brandy stopped him. "Taylor, you're in the hospital in the ICU unit," she informed him. She pressed a button to raise the head of the bed slightly. "My name is Brandy, and I need you to stay calm and try to lie still."

Taylor's eyes fell on his mother. "You were in a car accident," she explained. "But you're going to be okay."

The confusion in Taylor's eyes turned to fear as his eyes shifted to Bryant. "You heard what Mom said," Bryant told him.

Taylor's eyes filled with tears as they begged Bryant for the truth.

"I promise," Bryant assured him. "You're going to be okay."

Chapter 35

The morning passed slowly. Minutes crept by like hours as they waited for Taylor's doctors to stop by. Samantha arrived at the hospital around nine. An ICU nurse walked in Taylor's room and told Bryant and Felicia that Samantha had buzzed to come in. Because the ICU rules only allowed two visitors at a time, Bryant told his mom he would go out so Samantha could come in and see Taylor. "I'm going downstairs to the cafeteria and grab a bite to eat," Bryant told Taylor. "Are you going to be okay while I'm gone?"

Taylor nodded yes.

Bryant kissed his mom on the forehead then walked out the room. He met Samantha coming in the intensive care unit and hugged her. "How is he?" she asked.

"He's alert, but still kind of groggy," Bryant answered.

"Is he talking?"

"A little bit."

"Thank God."

"I'm going downstairs to the cafeteria," Bryant told her. "Call me if the doctor comes in before I get back."

"I will," Samantha replied then started toward Taylor's room.

Bryant pressed the button on the wall to open the doors, then he walked out and down the hallway to the elevators. He had not eaten anything since the pack of peanut butter crackers he bought from the vending machine last night, so he was glad there were only three people in the line ahead of him in the cafeteria. He ordered a waffle, scrambled eggs, hash browns, and link sausages. He fixed a cup of coffee, placed it on his tray, then sat down to enjoy his breakfast. He was on his second bite when he thought about Cassie and his promise to wait for her at Pearlie's Mae Café on Christmas Eve. When he flew into Chicago last night, he was worried about Taylor. Now that he had spoken to his brother and believed he would be all right, there was no way for him to avoid thinking about Cassie and how he had spent the past two Christmas Eves waiting for her at the café. He didn't want to waste another Christmas Eve waiting for her at the cafe, especially since Mr. Jake wouldn't be there and she wasn't coming. He did want to stop by the café and see Mr. Jake's niece Shirley, but since he was going to be home until after the new year, he thought it would be better to go another day instead of today – Christmas Eve. That way, he felt, stopping by the café would have nothing to do with waiting for Cassie.

It was almost noon when Taylor's surgeon, Dr. Ghai, finished his two scheduled surgeries and stopped by the intensive care unit to check on his patients. Dr. Ghai, a tall, slender Asian man, who looked a lot younger than his forty-six years, stopped at the nurse station and talked to Brandy while he looked over Taylor's chart. Felicia and Bryant watched from Taylor's room. Dr. Ghai and then Brandy entered the room.

"Taylor, I'm Dr. Ghai, the surgeon who operated on you when you were brought in yesterday," Dr. Ghai introduced himself. "I just reviewed your charts, and everything looks good. How do you feel?"

"Not too good," Taylor answered.

"Then that's pretty good considering what you've been through." Dr. Ghai smiled and began examining the fluid drain in Taylor's chest. "I know you don't want to spend your Christmas in the ICU, but I want to keep you here today and tomorrow so we can keep a real close eye on your drain," Dr. Ghai told Taylor. "We can probably move you to a regular room after tomorrow."

Felicia, who had been holding her breath while waiting for the prognosis, breathed a sigh of relief. "Thank you," she whispered to the Heavens. "Thank you." Bryant put his arm around his mother then silently thanked God.

"I'll be back to check on you," Dr. Ghai told Taylor.

"Thank you," Taylor said, his voice much stronger than it was earlier that morning.

Dr. Ghai and Brandy walked out the room.

Bryant walked up to Taylor's bed. "Now that I know you're going to be all right, I'm going to the house, take a shower, and change and while Mom, Talia, and Samantha are all here," he said. "I promise I won't be gone long."

"You don't have to worry about spending the night with him tonight," Felicia said. "I'm staying."

"No, you're not," Bryant countered. "They don't normally allow family members to stay in ICU rooms overnight. You have to stay in the waiting room. They allowed me to be in here last night so I could calm him down if he woke up and panicked."

"No," Taylor agreed. "Bryant's staying."

"You can take my car," Felicia offered and reached in her pocketbook for the keys.

"Thanks," Bryant said. She handed him the keys and he started out the room.

"Cassie," Taylor said.

Bryant turned around. "What about Cassie?"

"Bring Cassie back with you," Taylor told him. Bryant didn't know how to respond. He looked at Taylor and tried to smile.

"Are you going to stop by the café?" Felicia asked.

"I hadn't planned to," he answered.

"You should," Taylor told him.

"He's right," Felicia said. "I know you, son. You'll regret you didn't, especially because you're here. Besides, the café's not too out the way."

"Maybe," Bryant said and walked out the room.

As he pulled out the hospital's parking lot in his mother's car, Bryant remembered what she had said. The café wasn't out of the way going from the hospital to the house. And, she was right. If he didn't stop by the café, he would regret it, especially now that he was in Chicago on Christmas Eve. So, he decided to stop by the café but only for a few minutes – an hour at the most. He turned right onto the two-lane street next to the hospital and headed toward the intersection. The stoplight was red. While waiting for the light to change, he considered what he would do when he got there. He was going to go inside and let Shirley know that he heard about Mr. Jake and express his condolences. Then he was going to ask her how Mabel was doing. If Shirley or Eddie, the cook he met last Christmas Eve, were not working, he figured he would have a seat in the same booth by the window and enjoy a cup of coffee as he reminisced about the last three Christmas Eves at the café. The stoplight changed from red to green.

The roads had been plowed, but ice and snow were starting to accumulate again. So, Bryant took his time turning onto the four-lane highway that would have taken him two blocks from his mother's house if he wasn't going by the café first. He turned on the radio. Nat King Cole's "The Christmas Song," his mother's favorite holiday song, was playing. He listened at first, but then he found himself singing along. Before the song ended, he had also found his Christmas spirit. Until that moment, he had not been in a holiday mood. He knew why. Instead of enjoying the holiday festivities with his family in Chicago, he was supposed to spend the majority of the holiday alone at his house in Atlanta. Taylor's accident changed that. Now, he was in Chicago, and although Taylor's situation dampened the holidays for everyone, the family was still together for Christmas.

He was driving up Malloy Street toward the café when the traffic slowed and then stopped like it had the day that he met Cassie four years ago. He could not see past the third car in front of him, so he could not guess how long the traffic would be stalled. The cafe was right down the street, so instead of waiting for the stalled traffic to move, he pulled off the street into a row of metered parking spaces. By the time he paid the meter fee with his debit card, the traffic was moving again. He started up the sidewalk toward Pearlie Mae's. He was approaching the intersection when he glanced across the street at the café and saw her. Cassie was sitting in the same booth by the window.

Bryant stopped at the corner and stared across the street at Cassie just like he had the day he first saw her. She looked so hurt and alone that day. He remembered feeling compelled to cross the street, go inside the café, and sit with her so she wouldn't feel so alone. Unlike that day, today she appeared to be waiting patiently for someone. When she looked up and saw him standing on the corner, her smile invited him over. The stoplight changed and he crossed the street. He was still staring at her when he opened the door and stepped inside Pearlie Mae's Café.

Shirley and a waitress he had not met greeted him with, "Welcome to Pearlie Mae's."

He looked above the door. The mistletoe was still there.

"Somebody's waiting for you," Shirley told him. "She's been here since we opened this morning."

He walked over to the booth and sat across from Cassie. The present he left for her with Mr. Jake last Christmas Eve was on the table. "Hi," he said.

"Hi," she responded. "I wasn't sure you would be here after you deactivated your Facebook page. I thought maybe you had moved on."

"I thought I would never see you again," he responded.

She began unwrapping the present. "Mr. Jake gave me this last Christmas Eve after you left, but I decided to wait until I saw you to open it."

"You were here last Christmas Eve?"

"Yes, but you had already left," she answered.

While watching her unwrap the present, Bryant noticed she wasn't wearing a wedding ring. When she saw the bottle of Good Girl perfume, she smiled and said, "I love this." She opened the perfume and sprayed a light mist on her wrist then asked, "What do you think?" He held her hand in his, then he leaned forward to smell the perfume. The smile crisscrossing his face answered her question.